Joseph Hansen

Joseph Hansen wrote nearly forty novels in the course of a long career, but is best known for the ground-breaking series of twelve Dave Brandstetter crime novels. Brandstetter was a pioneering character: a tough private eye and happily uncloseted gay man. Hansen was an active campaigner for equal rights (though he disliked the word "gay" and always described himself as "homosexual"). He founded the pioneering gay journal *Tangents* in 1965, hosted a radio show called *Homosexuality Today*, and was involved in setting up the first Gay Pride parade in Hollywood in 1970, the same year that the first Brandstetter novel was published. In 1992, he won a Lifetime Achievement Award from the Private Eye Writers of America. He died in 2004.

JOSEPH HANSEN

Troublemaker

**MULHOLLAND
BOOKS**

HODDER

This paperback edition first published in Great Britain in
2015 by Mulholland Books
An imprint of Hodder & Stoughton
An Hachette UK company

I

Copyright © Joseph Hansen 1975

A CIP catalogue record for this title is available from the
British Library

Paperback ISBN 978 1 444 78451 0
eBook ISBN 978 1 444 78450 3

Typeset in Plantin Light by
Palimpsest Book Production Ltd, Falkirk, Stirlingshire

Printed and bound by Clays Ltd, St Ives plc

Hodder & Stoughton policy is to use papers that are natural,
renewable and recyclable products and made from wood
grown in sustainable forests. The logging and manufacturing
processes are expected to conform to the environmental
regulations of the country of origin.

Hodder & Stoughton Ltd
338 Euston Road
London NW1 3BH

www.hodder.co.uk

Troublemaker

I

She wore jeans, high-top work shoes, an old pullover with a jagged reindeer pattern. Somebody's ski sweater once, somebody even bigger than she was. Her son? She was sixty but there was nothing frail about her. The hands gripping the grainy rake handle were a man's hands. Her cropped hair was white. She wore no makeup. Her skin was ruddy, her eyes bright blue. *Hearty* might have described her. Except for her mouth. It sulked. Something had offended her and failed to apologize. Not lately—long ago. Life, probably.

He said, "Mrs. Wendell?" and held out a card. She took it, read it. It named the insurance company he worked for, Medallion Life. His own name, David Brandstetter, was in a corner, DEATH CLAIMS DIVISION under it. He didn't try to say it. His throat was dry. The morning was hot. It had been a hike from Pinyon Trail up crooked steps in a steep, pine-grown slope—rusty needles slippery underfoot—to the rambling redwood house where no one answered the bell, then out back here to this one-time garage.

It was a kind of stable now. Beside it, in pine-branch-splintered sunlight, a sorrel gelding no longer young nosed a heap of alfalfa back of an unpainted paddock fence. A cleated board ramp fronted the garage doors, canted to reach a wood floor laid on studs over the original cement. Inside, Heather Wendell raked manure and trampled straw out of a stall. In farther stalls, shadowy horses breathed and shifted hoofs on hollow planks. The big woman pushed the card into a pocket, turned away, went on with her work.

"Murders," she said, "inquests, grief. They don't mean anything to horses." It was a man's voice. Not pleased. "What is it you want?"

"Your son, Richard, had a policy with us."

"At my insistence." She jerked a nod, grim but self-satisfied. "He'd never have thought of it. It wasn't that he was selfish. He simply had no imagination. It never entered his head that he could die. I'd be destitute today. Well, I've had that, thank you. From my father. I wasn't going through it again. Not at my time of life." Her thick elbow nudged Dave. "Excuse me." She raked the pile past his feet, paused, blinked at him. "You've brought the check—is that it?"

"Wrong department." Dave smiled apology. "My department asks questions."

She grunted and began raking again, out into the light. She traded the rake for a stump of broom and pushed the waste off the ramp to the side. "There were a dozen police officers, in and out of uniform. That night, the next day. At least half of them asked questions. The same questions. Over and over again."

She leaned the broom beside the rake against a stud-and-board wall. Above sawhorses that held saddles, a tangle of tack trailed from rusty spikes. She took down a bridle and carried it to the stall beyond the one she'd cleaned. A bit clinked against teeth, a buckle tongue snapped. She led out a little paint mare who threw her head and blew when she saw Dave.

"Step back in there a minute, would you? Men make Buffy nervous. Thank you."

She held the sidling Buffy by a cheek strap and shouldered her out the door. Rusty hinges creaked on the paddock gate. It closed with a wooden clatter. She came back in and took the rake to Buffy's stall.

"I assume one of those officers was bright enough to write. That Japanese one, surely. Or don't the police let insurance companies see their reports?"

"Lieutenant Yoshiba," Dave said. "I saw the report."

"Good. Then there's no need to waste your morning. Nor mine. These horses haven't been groomed or exercised in days. That's not right. And I'm pressed for time. The funeral's this afternoon."

"You'd gone to a film that night," Dave said. "In Los Santos. Left here a little after seven. The film screened at eight and ran three hours but you were back here before ten and it's a forty-minute drive. What happened?"

"I walked out. The movie was disgusting. They're all like that now—cruel, bloody, degenerate. I tried to make myself stay, it cost so much to get in. And Rick keeps telling me I'm letting myself get old, stuck away up here, that I ought to get out in civilization once in a while." The rake clunked at the back of the dark stall. She snorted. "Civilization! Do you know what they do to horses in those pictures? The S.P.C.A. here in the States won't let them use trip wires—you know, to make them

3

stumble and fall. But they go out of the country now to film, and they don't care. They break their legs, their necks, kill them. To make a cheap, sordid movie. Don't talk to me about civilization."

"I won't," Dave said. "You got home around ten?"

"Parked the car where I always do. Down below, by the mailbox. You can see we don't use the garage for cars anymore." The rake quit a moment while she jerked a thumb over her shoulder. "When we did, we drove down from the trail above—same trail but it climbs and bends back on itself. Only take horses up and down the driveway now. Hardly a patch of blacktop left on it. Anyway, the climb up the steps is good exercise. My father always said, 'Walking is for horses,' and he died at forty-nine."

"Right," Dave said. "You heard a shot?"

"When I was partway up the stairs. Didn't know what it was. Sounded like a backfire from down on the main road. These hills echo so. And my mind wasn't on it. I was furious about that movie." Now she backed past Dave again, dragging the litter from Buffy's stall with the rake. "I set some milk in a pan on the stove to heat. To calm me down, let me sleep. I thought I'd change for bed while it warmed up and I started for my room. And I saw across the way there was a light in Rick's den. That wasn't right—he was at work. Then I remembered his VW was down by the mailbox when I'd parked. Shows you how that movie upset me. Normally he doesn't get home till three." She added without pride, "It's a bar he owns, you know. With Ace Kegan."

4

"The Hang Ten," Dave said. "A gay bar. On Ocean Front Walk in Surf."

"Yes." She eyed him thoughtfully for a second, then went on scraping the stall muck toward the sunlit doorway. "Well, I was afraid Rick must be ill. I thought I'd better step across and check. It's a separate unit, you understand. It was a guesthouse originally—two bedrooms and bath. Rick remodeled one room so as to have a place where he could relax, listen to music, watch TV and not disturb me. Our hours are different. Were. The door was open. And there was this boy, this creature—what's his name?—Johns. Standing at the desk, stark naked, tissues in his hand, wiping off a revolver. While my son lay dead at his feet."

"Also stark naked," Dave said.

"No." She stopped in the doorway, a bulky silhouette, and raised her head. Against the light, he couldn't read her expression. But her voice changed. It belonged to an old woman now. "There was a great, gaping hole in his chest. I remember that. Was he naked? Yes." Her shoulders sagged. "I suppose he was."

"Can I see that room?" Dave asked.

"The police took photographs." The rake handle knocked the wall. She broomed the dirty straw. Angry now. Probably at herself for showing human weakness. "They left the fireplace littered with those ugly little burned-out bulbs."

"I've seen the photographs," Dave said. "Now I need to see the room. Don't stop what you're doing. Just point me the way." Wincing against the hard light, he started down the ramp.

She squared herself in front of him. "I'm not sure I have to do that. What is it you want here? No—don't bother to lie. I know insurance companies. I got acquainted with them in 1937. When all the policies my father had kept up for years were canceled. Because he'd missed some payments at the end. When he was helplessly ill. You'd like to find a way to stop my getting the money my son meant for me to have. To go on with. Lord knows, twenty-five thousand is little enough these days. Would you care to try to live the rest of your life on that amount?"

"No," Dave said. "There's going to be a delay, though, Mrs. Wendell. Till after the trial. You understand that."

She stared. "Indeed I do not. Why? The police know that boy did it. The district attorney knows."

"A jury has to know," Dave said. "Beyond a reasonable doubt. And juries aren't predictable."

"But there he stood with the gun!" she cried. "The gun that killed my son." Her lip trembled and she bit it sharply.

"Your son's own gun, wasn't it? You told the police he kept it in his desk."

"Hippies infest this canyon." She stepped past him into the stable dark. Tack jingled. She was taking another bridle off its nail. "We're isolated up here. Help's a long way off. Nowhere, if the telephone's out. And that happens, you know." Her work shoes thumped the planks. Her voice came muffled from the back of the stable. "Los Santos hasn't the most up-to-date equipment. A rainstorm, a Santana— it breaks down." A small window showed grimy light above the farthest stall. He saw her lifted hands work the bridle over a big, dark muzzle. "It would be foolish not to keep a gun up here."

"Guns are for television actors," Dave said. "Not real people. The wrong ones always get hurt. Your son could be alive this morning."

She didn't answer. She spoke to the horse, coaxing, soft. Hoofs came on, a halting stumble. Dave stepped down onto the pine-needle mat of the yard and watched her steer this one into the paddock. Ganted, knob-kneed, mane and tail stringy. The sun showed newly healed scars along sides and flanks. A rip between the eyes was still jagged and red. Heather Wendell closed the gate and over it stroked a hammer head. "Beaten with barbwire," she said. "By a crazy man. The county would have destroyed him. Not the man—oh, never. The horse. I couldn't let them do that. He'll be all right soon." There was crooning tenderness in the words. Not for Dave. For the horse. She turned to face Dave again and he told her:

"It's not the only thing, but the gun worries me. The jury's going to snag on it too. A police lab man will tell them there were powder burns on your son's hand. And his chest. It was fired point-blank. They could come up with suicide."

"But the coroner's jury didn't say so."

"They said Johns had to stand trial. That's all. It doesn't bind the jury that will hear his case. They won't even know about it. And if they acquit Johns, it complicates things for my company. If Richard Wendell took his own life, we can't pay. It's in the policy."

"Yes." Her mouth twisted in a sour smile. "And that would suit your company, wouldn't it?" She bunched her fists. "Well, it won't happen. It's not common sense. A man doesn't commit suicide with someone else present. A stranger." She stepped toward Dave and her words came like thrown rocks. "The explanation for the powder burns is obvious. Rick was holding the gun. Probably found the boy trying to steal. They struggled. The gun went off. Right against Rick's chest."

"Maybe," Dave said. "Johns tells it a little differently." The sun beat down. Dave shed his jacket, hung it over an arm. "He claims they were in bed and Richard Wendell heard a sound in the den. He went to investigate. Johns heard voices—your son's, another man's—and a shot. He was frightened and it took him a minute to move. When he came out of the bedroom, your son lay on the floor. He bent over him, shook him. No sign of life. Blood. The gun. He picked it up because he was too dazed to be careful. Then he realized he'd made a mistake and what he had to do was wipe his prints off it, get his clothes and run. Only the clock ran out on him. You walked in."

"And took the gun away from him." Her mouth twitched contempt. "Six feet tall, one of those long mustaches, long hair. He cried like a girl, begged, pleaded. Oh, I heard his story. Half a dozen times while we waited for the police." Her laugh was brief and scornful. "Lies. Pointless. He killed Rick."

"For money?" Dave asked. "Your son's wallet lay

8

on the chest in his bedroom, undisturbed. Two hundred dollars in it. Ones, fives, tens, twenties."

"In case they ran short of change at The Hang Ten," she said. "He always carried it. Of course it was there. The boy hadn't taken it because there wasn't time. I interrupted him."

"What about the open door?" Dave said. She looked blank and he told her, "You found the door open, remember? What they were doing they wouldn't leave the door open for, would they? They wouldn't only have closed it, they'd have locked it."

"There's no lock," she said. "There is—but there's no key. And the spring lock's painted shut. This is an old place. When we bought it, there wasn't any need for locks up here. Too remote. And we had Homer, our big Dane. Dead now."

"But it was standing open," Dave said. "That's going to help Johns's defense."

"He has no defense," she said flatly. "He'd opened it himself and left it open and Rick heard him out there and came out and—"

"Naked?" Dave said gently.

"I don't know what that means," she said, "but he's a hippie. They're all over up here. Why hadn't he wandered in? Who knows what goes on in their heads? It's common knowledge they've ruined their minds with drugs. He didn't come by car. At least the police haven't found a car."

"He says your son picked him up and brought him here," Dave said. "And his clothes weren't in the den, Mrs. Wendell. They were in the bedroom."

She opened her mouth and shut it hard and

turned to tramp off up the board slope into the stable. "I have work to do." When she came out, her big fingers clasped a square wood-backed brush, a coarse-toothed metal comb that glinted in the sunlight. She let herself into the paddock and began working on the sorrel.

Dave walked to the fence, put a foot up on the lowest bar, crossed his arms on the top bar and rested his chin on them. "I went to the theater last night," he said. "In Los Santos. Talked to the night crew. You're not somebody who'd go unnoticed, Mrs. Wendell. Nobody remembers seeing you."

The brush stopped its motion. She turned. "Mr. Brandstetter, my fingerprints are also the only ones on that gun. Neither circumstance means anything. Since you don't appear to have the wit to see that, I shall explain it to you. My son earned twelve to fourteen thousand dollars a year. Gave me a roof over my head, clothes for my back, food to eat. He let me indulge my hobby, which is an expensive one. Not without protest—but he never in the end denied me anything. Now . . . why would I kill him? For twenty-five thousand dollars insurance money?"

"It doesn't add up," Dave admitted. "Neither does anything else about this case. That's what bothers me." He sighed, straightened, turned from the fence. "But it will. It will." He looked down at the gray shake roofs tree-shadowed below. "Are those his rooms, in the L of the house there?"

2

She didn't answer and he went down broken flag steps between terraced beds where wild oats, passion vine, sunflowers choked out iris, carnations, nasturtiums, and where fat white roses strewed cankered petals from neglected canes. A lizard scuttled ahead of him down the mossy passage between house and guesthouse and lost itself in a rattle of dry leaves among flowerpots where leggy geraniums withered. She'd gardened last year. There must have been fewer horses then.

The guesthouse door had square glass panes, a reed blind on the inside. He turned the knob, which was faceted, paint-specked glass, and went in. Richard Wendell had used lumberyard bargain birch paneling on the walls. Modular shelves held stereo equipment, a portable television set, a slide projector, records, books, stacks of magazines. The carpeting was mottled blue green. So were the curtains.

At the room's near end, basket chairs faced a fireplace. At the far end, a blue couch looked at windows that framed ferns and the trunks of big pines. The windows stood open. They had square panes too and went out on hinges and stayed out by means of long rods hooked through eyes dense with old paint. The screens were on the inside. A little light desk backed the couch. Next to the desk the carpet had been scrubbed and was still wet. Papers littered the desk.

There were bills, subscription blanks, an opened gaudy advertisement for a book about Renaissance Italy, with off-register reproductions of famous paintings. Blue Kleenex poked up out of a wooden housing meant to hide the box. A ballpoint pen stamped in cheap gilt THE HANG TEN lay by a brown envelope. On the back of the envelope somebody had worked arithmetic problems, taking percentages of twenty-five thousand. Heather Wendell must have sat here last night sweating out her prospects. At a passbook five and a quarter percent, she'd about be able to feed the horses.

He opened a shallow center drawer. Stamps, paper clips, rubber bands, address labels in a little plastic box, pencils, more of the souvenir pens. He opened side drawer left. Envelopes, writing paper, an address book in fake leather. He lifted these out. Underneath was a scatter of little Kodachrome slides. He held one up to the light. Naked boys in a basic sex position. He tried some others. Same boys but the positions changed. He dropped them back and laid the stationery on them.

The address book had letter tabs along the page edges. He picked the letter J. There were three names that meant nothing to him. But at the bottom of the page were two numbers unattached to any name. One had been scratched out. He looked for a telephone. It crouched on a low shelf by a cluster of brown-glazed clay pots. Handsome. The kind that came out of local kilns. The kind Doug Sawyer's new shop was waist deep in. Most of those had been thrown by a lank, bushy-haired youth named Kovaks. Dave shrugged Kovaks away. He was going to mean trouble but he wasn't trouble yet and right now Dave had work to do. He dialed the number.

It rang once and the connection opened with a crash and dogs barked into his ear. He flinched and held the receiver away. A girl's voice scolded the dogs and yelped, "Hello?" The dogs kept barking. The girl called, "Will you please get them out of here?" Someone swore. The dogs barked. A door slammed. Silence.

Dave asked, "To whom am I speaking?"

"To whom did you want to speak?" Quick, sweet and wary. This wasn't some kid he could con information out of. He'd better cut his losses.

"Larry Johns," he said.

"I'm sorry, he's not here now."

Dave felt himself grin. The only address the Los Santos police had for Larry Johns was off his driver's license. A cheap hotel in Brownsville, Texas, the kind of place that didn't know where you'd come from or where you'd gone. Especially not if it was the law asking. Where Larry Johns had gone was, of course, Los Santos, a quiet town that clambered the tree-green oceanside hills northwest of L.A. But small as it was, Los Santos had thousands of street numbers. And Larry Johns wasn't telling which was his. Why didn't seem to interest Lieutenant Tek Yoshiba. It interested Dave. He said carefully, "When do you expect him?"

She did it again—answered a question with a question. Sweetly. "Who's calling, please?"

He told her and she asked him to wait and he waited, watching a bluejay hammer a pine cone on a rock outside the windows. Then someone picked up an extension. A male voice said, "What about insurance? I've got insurance. I'm collecting on it right now."

"I'm not selling it," Dave said. "I'm trying to reach Larry Johns. Does he live there?"

There were five dead seconds. "How the hell did you get this number?" Back of him, women exchanged loud words in a place that echoed. Heels clacked.

Dave said, "It's in Richard Wendell's book."

"Oh, Christ," the man groaned. Then he said sharply, "No, Gail, wait!" And a female spoke into the phone. Not the one who'd answered first, with the dogs. This voice was older. "You have the wrong number," it said, and the receiver slammed. But only on the extension. On the other phone he heard remote man-woman shouts. Then the dogs barked again. The heels neared. The connection broke. He hung up.

He'd lapped his jacket over the back of the desk chair. Out of it he dug a small notebook and checked a number he kept there. Dialing it got him Ray Lollard at the central office of Pacific Telephone. Lollard was a plump, feminine man who collected antiques and had been a friend of Rod Fleming, a decorator Dave used to live with, who had died last fall. Rod had restored an old mansion—porches, cupolas, stained glass—on West Adams for Lollard. It was a showplace.

"Davey!" Lollard sounded pleased but he always sounded pleased. "I keep thinking we'll run into each other at Romano's." He meant the West Los Angeles restaurant where they'd met in 1948. "But it seems you don't eat these days. Rod always said you'd starve to death if he didn't remind you. But of course, that's how you keep that elegant figure."

"We'll set a date," Dave said. "Listen, Ray—find out who owns this number." He gave it. "If you can get it for me in say ten minutes, call me back here." He read Richard Wendell's number off the dial plaque.

"Pleasure," Lollard said. "How are you? How's Doug? Happy? The new gallery flourishing, is it?"

"He's lonely," Dave said. "Try to get around there, will you? None of it's old but he's got some really beautiful stuff. And he needs customers."

"I gather *you* don't lack for customers."

"People keep dying," Dave said. "Look, if I don't hear from you, I'll get back to you later. I don't know just where I'm headed."

Lollard said something amiable that amounted to nothing. So did Dave. He hung up and went back to the desk, frowning. The envelope with the figuring on it was tough and bulky. He turned it over. *Security Bank, 132 Pier Street, Los Santos* was in the upper-left-hand corner. That was all. No addressee. It hadn't gone through any mail. And it wasn't quite empty. Inside, his fingers found three paper straps, each with "$500" rubber-stamped on it. He glanced at the phone but he didn't have a friend at Security Bank's central office. He'd have to go through channels. He tucked the straps into a jacket pocket.

The right-hand desk drawer was an indifferent shambles of canceled checks, paid bills, tax forms, wish-you-were-here postcards, snapshots. He thumbed through these. Most were of the sorrel horse and a harlequin Great Dane. A couple caught Heather Wendell sitting the horse or holding the dog's leash. Here was a big, grinning young man leaning against a car. As that ski sweater had suggested, a giant.

At the back of the drawer were red, silver and blue rosetted ribbons. *Los Santos Dog Show*: 1950s, 1960s. On the bottom of the drawer lay a yellowing eight-by-ten glossy of a dark, curly-haired little youth in boxing trunks. He scowled above raised fists that were wrapped in gauze. Across the picture's lower corner an ungifted penman had written: *To Rick—All My Love—Ace*. Dave laid the picture back and covered it up again with the waste paper of Rick Wendell's life.

Suits, pants, jackets off the X-large rack hung in the bedroom closet. Big towels lay wadded on the checkerboard tiles of the bathroom floor. The shower dripped behind a plastic curtain. The bed was a scrimmage of creased sheets. The blankets had half fallen to the floor. By the head of the bed was an eight-millimeter projector with reels on it. Facing the bed foot, a spring-roller screen glittered on a metal tripod. Dave drew the blue-green curtains across the windows and flipped the projector switch.

On the screen boys naked except for cowboy hats, gun belts and tooled boots had sex with each other on what looked like a Baja beach. Some such sunburned place. Sweat stuck sand to their pale city skins. They acted bored. Dave snapped off the projector, opened the curtains, walked around the bed, looking at the floor. A comb, a leather packet of keys, a dime and two pennies. And a pair of Jockey shorts. He picked them up. Size 32. No giant's. He dropped them and something changed the light in the room. He looked at the door.

A giant stood there, a big-boned old man. His thick gray hair needed cutting. His cheap suit needed pressing. The white shirt, the black tie, looked as if they'd just been bought, though. And he'd used a lot of polish to fill the cracks in the uppers of his shoes. Dave smelled Shinola. The man's eyes were pouchy and the skin over his cheekbones and nose was a river map of small broken veins. But a carefully tended mustache said he'd been vain once. He asked, "Who are you?"

"Brandstetter," Dave said. "Medallion Life." He held out his hand. The man folded it in a grip that had long ago given up trying to hold on to anything.

"This is the Wendell house, isn't it?" He licked dry, cracked lips and his bloodshot eyes fidgeted around the room. Looking for something. A drink, probably.

"It's the Wendell house," Dave said. "I'm trying to find out what happened here."

"Thought the police had the son of a bitch locked up." The man turned back into the living room.

Dave rounded the bed and went after him. He was opening cabinet doors below the modular shelving. He found a bottle and glasses. "Join me?" He lifted them at Dave. "I'm Billy Wendell. Rick's father. I don't think he'd mind his old man having a blast, do you?"

"It's a little late to ask him," Dave said. "Don't you know?"

"Hadn't seen him for a while." Wendell poured three thick fingers into a glass and handed it to Dave and poured five for himself and set the bottle down. "His mother and I weren't speaking." He jerked his long jaw up in silent ironic laughter. "Not for some years." He drank, studied his glass, looked at Dave. "Insurance, huh? That's a good racket. I was in it once." He made an unamused sound and drank again. "I was in about everything once. But it's been used cars lately. Lately? Last twenty years. Now it's dying under me. You don't need a gas hog, do you?" He handed Dave a card, looked him up and down. "You don't look like money gives you bad dreams."

"I drive a company car," Dave said. "You've come back for the funeral, right?"

Wendell nodded. His voice went to pieces. Tears leaked down his face. "My boy. My only son. Jesus— least I could do. Poor kid. Not forty years old yet and some crazy pervert murders him." He wagged his head. "The one thing I could be a little bit proud of—fine son." He gulped the last of his drink.

"Sure," Dave said. "How did you find out about it? Your wife write to you?"

"Hell, she wouldn't know where to reach me. No, I saw it on television. The *Times* was where I got the address. Had to look sharp to find it. Guess there are too many murders anymore for it to be news."

"There were always too many," Dave said. "You live in L.A., then?"

"Torrance," Billy Wendell said. "If you could call it living." He set down the glass where it would make a mark in the finish. "Is there a bathroom?"

Dave jerked his head. Wendell went out, moving his long legs as if they pained him. Dave checked his watch, looked at the phone. It didn't ring. He tasted the whiskey, walked to the bottle and turned it so the label showed. Right. They didn't cart this in by the truckload for the bar. He rummaged his jacket for a cigarette, lit it with a narrow steel butane lighter, and the scuff of clumsy shoes outside turned his head toward the door. Heather Wendell stopped there, the withering geraniums flaring red behind her.

"You see, Mr. Brandstetter, I know about death. It's not the dead we ought to mourn for. It's the living. When my father died, his troubles were over. Mine had only started. I was twenty-five—a grown woman. But he'd sheltered me like a child. I'd never had to lift a hand. Everything I'd needed or imagined I needed was given me. Then suddenly it was all taken away. I had nothing. And a three-year-old boy to raise."

"You had a husband," Dave said.

She shook her head. "When the money stopped, he left. He was no better equipped to face reality than I was. It was no surprise to me." The corner of her mouth tightened in a kind of smile. "Do you know how I managed? By doing for a living exactly what you found me doing this morning—cleaning stables, grooming horses. Horses were all I knew. Then came the war and the aircraft factories. They hired women because women were what there were to hire. Whether they knew anything or not. I bucked rivets for four years." The crooked smile tried itself again and failed. "Well, you don't want to hear the rest. I don't want to remember it. At last Rick took hold and my nightmare was over." Her shoulders lifted a little, as if shedding the weight all over again. "Naturally, if I'd had my choice, it wouldn't have been the kind of business it was. But I didn't have my choice, did I? Come to think of it, never once in my life did I choose—"

The toilet flushed. She frowned puzzlement at the bedroom door. Dave picked up his drink and tasted it again and Billy Wendell came in, zipping a fly that didn't work well. He stopped, blinked.

"Heather," he said heavily.

She squinted, head craning forward. "Billy?" She took a step into the room, a hand half held out. "Dear God—what's happened to you?"

"Happened?" he said. "I'm sixty-five years old."

"I'm sorry," she said. "It's such a shock is all. Where did you come from?" She looked at him, grieved.

"Not far." He made for his glass like a drowning man for a piece of driftwood. He gulped from it, wiped his mustache with the back of his hand. "You want a drink? It's your booze."

"You mean you've been close by"—she didn't say it angry, she said it sad—"and never come around, never shown your face?"

"I didn't know where you'd got to." He bent creakily for another glass. "Not till I read about Rick in the paper." He dumped whiskey into the glass, set the bottle by, carried the glass to her. "You landed on your feet. Pleasant place here, nice furnishings." He tilted his head. "Portrait of you on the wall in there, with a big dog." He looked her up and down as he'd done Dave, smiled to himself as he walked back to put more whiskey into his glass. He was wasting a beautiful bottle in a hurry. "Horses again, eh? You know"—he drank—"I'm happy about that. I was afraid you'd never have them anymore. Costs a lot of money to keep horses."

"You worried about me?" What she wanted in her smile was disbelief but her damp eyes showed she was touched. "I worried about you, Billy."

"You had a right," he grunted. Back to her, he opened the top magazine in a stack on a shelf. Dave caught a glimpse of naked male bodies. In color. Billy Wendell shut the magazine fast. He turned to face his wife. "*I* didn't land on my feet. Charm and good looks weren't in a seller's market in those days. By the time they were, I was an old wreck."

"No," she protested gently. "Ah, Billy. There's so much to talk about." She glanced back at the open door, the morning light. "Will you come with me? To the stable up the hill?"

Dave said, "In a minute, Mrs. Wendell." He picked up his jacket, dug out the flattened paper straps.

"These were in that empty envelope on the desk. From the bank." He laid them in her hand. "What do they mean? Where's the fifteen hundred?"

She frowned at the straps, then at him. "Fifteen—" She paled, then reddened. "That damned boy!"

"He was naked, remember?" Dave said and took back the straps. "Each of these held twenty-five twenty-dollar bills. They'd make a bulge even if he'd had pockets."

"Then—" She looked at her hand as if surprised to find the glass there. She drank from it. Her blue eyes on Dave's were uncertain. "It—it must have gone with Rick to the bar. Of course."

"Out of the envelope?" Dave said.

"Obviously," she said.

"All right." Dave shrugged into the jacket. "Thanks for your help." He went to the desk for the envelope, tucked the straps into it, held it up. "I'll take this if it won't inconvenience you."

For a moment she looked doubtful. Then she shrugged. "Why not?"

"Why not?" Billy Wendell said. Loudly but to himself, rattling bottle against glass. Then softly. "Why not? That's what I say. What does anything matter now? Rick's dead. My son's dead." He turned toward his wife and the tears were streaming now.

"Billy, Billy!" She went toward him with her arms held out. Big strong arms he'd made a mistake ever to leave. They embraced him, held him.

Dave went out into the sun.

Ace Kegan said, "It's a hassle to change names."

The years had taken the curl and most of the black out of his hair and there wasn't a lot of it left. What there was he combed forward into bangs. His waist had thickened but he still looked hard and muscular. He stood shirtless and barefoot in faded Levi's and watched through open glass slide doors while outside on a slatted deck a slender suntanned kid of maybe eighteen in very short shorts fisted a punching bag on a shiny spring-steel pole. His shoulder-length yellow hair flopped. He had a silky yellow mandarin mustache. Backgrounding him, the Pacific wrote white scribbles to itself on a blue slate under a wide smile of sky. The surf lipped pale sand beyond a stagger of red dune fences.

Kegan went on, "I'd have liked to take The Square Circle with me when we bought the place. But what the hell, who knows boxing down here? Down here it's surfing. And the Hang Ten sign was already there and neon costs like you wouldn't believe. Anyway, fags aren't into prize fighting." His sidelong grin at Dave showed chipped teeth that were very white. His nose was mashed. Scar tissue was thick over his eyes. An ear was crumpled. He still managed to be handsome. Dave let himself grin back.

"Are they into surfing?"

"Into surfers"—Kegan laughed—"they wish." He raised his sandpaper voice. "Bobby, come in here and make the man and me a drink." He took Dave's elbow and steered him among barbells, a rowing machine, an Exercycle, to a couch that was long and low and covered in white fake fur. "Sit down, Mr. Brandstetter. What did you want to know?"

Dave said, "What excuse did Richard Wendell give you for not being at work that night—Monday?"

"He *was* at work," Kegan said. "Half an hour early: three-thirty. He didn't split till nearly eight." He told the boy, "On the double, Bobby, please," and dropped onto the other end of the couch. "What'll you have to drink?"

"Whatever you're having," Dave said, hoping for coffee. But what the boy brought from the kitchen beyond a chest-high room divider banked with plastic flowers was a tall, thick, creamy mixture colored orange. Kegan took a long gulp of his and smacked his lips. Dave watched him, doubtful. "Go ahead, try it. Every vitamin and mineral you can name. One glass and you can go fifteen stand-up rounds." Bobby stood in front of them, straddling barbells and staring at Dave's glass with wistful, empty brown eyes. Kegan asked him, "Right, baby?"

"Aw, shit," Bobby said. "A piece of dry toast and black coffee for breakfast. I'm hungry, Ace."

"Yeah, and you're also a lard collector. You know what it does to you. Bobby Reich, shake hands with

David Brandstetter. Check his build. I'll bet he doesn't even eat breakfast." Ace turned over a thick wrist to check a multidialed watch. "Go run for half an hour. But when you get to the pier, keep away from the chili dogs, right? I got you looking like Apollo Belvedere now. Don't wreck it before the big night."

"Yeah, okay." Bobby headed eagerly for the door.

"And no Cokes, either. None of that lousy sugar water. When you get back here, I'll build you a salad, broil you a steak."

"Gee, thanks." Bobby made a six-year-old's face.

"You'll thank me when you walk off with all the marbles," Ace said. "You got T. S. Eliot this afternoon, remember? Before we hit the funeral. And *La Bohème* after. Did you read about Puccini last night, like I said?"

"I fell asleep," Bobby answered.

"Yeah," Ace said. "'I wake to sleep and take my waking slow.' Recite that on your way."

"Jesus!" the blond youth said and left.

"That's a Theodore Roethke poem," Dave said. "What kind of boxer are you trying to make?"

"Boxer! Bobby?" Kegan laughed, shook his head and downed more of the orange-color drink. "That's very funny. No, it's for the Mr. Marvelous contest. Between the gay bars. Each one puts up a beautiful kid. But he's also got to have something in his head, you know? Culture?"

"Correct his handshake," Dave said. "People with limp handshakes are takers."

"He only did it not to hurt you," Ace said. "Don't worry about me. Nobody takes Ace Kegan."

"Somebody took Richard Wendell," Dave said.

Kegan looked morose. "Yeah. All the way down." He nodded at the doors through which Bobby had vanished. "You think that kid is dumb? You should have known Rick. Only he was big and stubborn and he wasn't any kid. Heather and I did our best to keep him grounded, but . . ." He let it trail away.

"How do you mean—grounded?" Dave didn't trust the drink. He set it on a low steel-legged glass table where magazines like *High Fidelity* and *The New Yorker* jostled comic books—*Batman, Creepy*—and where the records were Stevie Wonder and a box of four Brahms symphonies. "Was it a question of odds? Did he take home a lot of boys like Larry Johns?"

"Hah!" Kegan got up and stepped over the exercise equipment to punch a button on a record changer. A German half-gram pickup slowly settled on a record. The same pianist played Erik Satie from four corners of the room at once. Kegan turned back. "That would have been no problem. I tried to get him on the bath circuit. In one night you can get enough sex for a year. I bought him memberships. He wouldn't go."

"He owned pictures, magazines, slides," Dave said.

"Yeah. Dependable. You turn on the projector, they're always the same. That was what he wanted, somebody permanent. Only what he picked—they'd never be. Talk about takers. Jesus—the last one!"

Weights on pulleys were steel-framed against a wall. Kegan began to haul on them, this arm, that arm, thick muscle sliding under the brown skin of his shoulders and upper back. "Mickey Something. I forget his last name. I never called him Mickey. I called him Monkey. That was what he looked like. Took Rick down to his socks. In about six weeks' time. I mean it." The pulleys squeaked. "Damn near wiped Rick out and me with him."

"When was this?"

"Three, four years back. Summer. Hot like this one. Long, hot summer. Maybe that was what did it."

"It might have been simpler," Dave said. "It might have been fifteen hundred dollars." Kegan let the weights crash and turned. Dave held up the brown envelope. "I stopped by the bank on my way here. He drew it on Monday, just before closing time—three."

"Yeah. Well—" A nerve twitched beside Kegan's eye. He scratched his belly, shifted his feet. "That was for—uh—for the bar. Alterations. Yeah. I forgot about that." He leaned across the table to take the envelope. He turned it over in clumsy fingers, staring at it. "Where's the bread?"

"That's what I came to ask you," Dave said. "I found the envelope on the desk in his den. Empty except for the straps that had held the bills. Twenties, I'd guess. Why should he get cash in small bills for alterations? Why not a business check?"

"Mmm." Kegan's tongue pushed at his shut mouth. Then he let go a helpless grin. "Okay. But understand—he was handling it. See, we're lowering the bar. No, raising the floor, really. So what we needed would be chairs, not stools. What we had in mind were barrel chairs on swivels, deep leather, you know? But they cost a lot. He must have got some deal right off the truck, you know? Lost shipment? You'd need cash for that kind of deal."

"You were his partner," Dave said.

Kegan looked at him hard and handed back the envelope. "I didn't know anything about it. Who got the money? The Johns kid?"

"There was a house key, three dollars and change in the pants the police found on Wendell's bedroom floor. A pack of cigarettes and a throwaway lighter in his shirt. The sarape didn't have pockets."

"What does Heather say?" Kegan picked up his empty glass and Dave's full one and took them to the kitchen. The smack of rubber stripping said he'd opened a refrigerator door. Ice cubes rattled into a glass. The door clapped shut. Kegan stood beside the flowers with what looked like whiskey in an Old Fashioned glass. Tasting it made him wince.

"She says it must have been for the bar."

"Yeah, well, like I said . . ." Kegan gave Dave a wan smile on his way to the doors to stand looking out. "Fifteen hundred. That hurts."

"Maybe Wendell delivered the money." Dave got up from the couch and went to stand by the short man. "Maybe the chairs will show up today."

Kegan shook his head. "That kind of deal, they get the bread when they turn over the goods." He looked at Dave. "Jesus, I'm a hell of a host. Here. This is for you. I don't even drink." He pushed the glass at Dave. "It's Canadian. All right?" Dave took it to keep it from falling. The breeze off the sea was warm. Sandpipers hemstitched the wet edge of the sand.

He said, "What happened with Monkey, exactly?"

"He walked into the bar out of nowhere—the way Savage did before him. Now, you have to understand Rick. Ten thousand guys come and go in our place. The Hang Ten and The Square Circle before that. Out of that number, some are on the hustle. And that big, soft bear—all you had to do was look at him to know he was a mark. And listen to him—talk, talk, talk. No secrets."

"If the weather was hot," Dave said.

"Yeah, well—" Kegan watched a gull swoop on a potato chip bag the wind was tumbling along the sparsely populated beach. "He could smile and talk and leave nine thousand nine hundred ninety-nine of them strictly alone. Then along would come a Monkey or a Savage and he'd be gone. Right out of his skull. And you never knew when it would be. You had to watch him. Every minute."

"How did Larry Johns get past?" Dave asked.

"I never heard of him," Kegan said, "till that night. We were on to Rick. But he was on to us, it looks like. Normally, he'd have yakked on and on about the kid. Not this time. Sneaky."

"'We'?" Dave said. "Meaning you and his mother?" Kegan nodded glumly and Dave tried the whiskey. Nice. "Maybe the fifteen hundred was for him—Johns. Another Monkey, another Savage. When was Savage?"

"Christ, who remembers? Maybe sixty-four, -five. See, years could go by. You could forget about it— what a jackpot Rick could turn into when he saw something he wanted. He gave Monkey a car, a new MG. Savage wanted to jet to Rome. They went together. For a month. For Monkey, Rick damn near sold the house in the canyon. I mean it. Heather would have been out on her ass. Monkey didn't like the place, the horses, the dog—and especially he didn't like Heather." Kegan's smile was wry. "Not that she made it any secret, how she felt about him."

"What stopped it?" Dave asked.

"The escrow took too long on the new place," Kegan said. "A condominium. By the marina. Way out of Rick's price class. But like I say, when he was what he called 'in love,' he couldn't count." Kegan lifted his hard shoulders, spread his hands. "Monkey must have just got tired of waiting. He took off in his MG and didn't come back. We lucked out. He'd wasted fifteen, twenty big bills by then— Rick's, mine, Heather's. It could have been thirty and—look, Ma, no business, no house, no partnership, no nothing." He closed flat hands under his armpits and shuddered. "Makes me sweat now to think of it. I mean, it was that close."

"It's that close now for Mrs. Wendell," Dave said. "The bank says he had less than two hundred in his savings account. With those horses to feed—"

"She's as big a mark as he is." Kegan stepped out on the deck and began tapping the punching bag. "That little paint horse? Came from some ten-year-old girl in the canyon. Her parents said she

30

could have it but only if she looked after it herself. Ten years old." He punched the bag hard. "Crazy. What did they really expect? So—they were going to sell it. But Heather stepped in, said she'd board it at her own expense and the little girl could come ride it when she wanted. Then that big, mud-color horse—"

"She told me about him," Dave said. "She's going to have to stop. All she's got now is the twenty-five thousand from Wendell's life insurance. If my company decides he didn't kill himself. Or that she didn't kill him."

"What!" Kegan stepped back from the lunging bag.

"Her prints are the only ones on the gun," Dave said. "The defense attorney will hammer on that."

"Christ." Disgusted, Kegan swung away to lean his fists on the rail. He turned back. "Why? Why would she kill Rick? Why not Johns?"

Dave shrugged. "Maybe she meant to kill Johns and her son tried to stop her and the gun went off."

Kegan put his hands on his hips. "Why would she want to kill anybody?"

"If she thought Johns was going to be another Monkey—to get rid of him. While she still had a roof over her head."

Mouth tight at one corner, Kegan gave his head a shake and went back to punching the bag. "You've got quite a mind."

"Will she inherit her son's partnership? That would solve her financial problems."

"Be serious." Kegan made a face but didn't break

the rhythm of his fists. "I need a working partner. You probably saw her in overalls but she's a very classy lady. She wouldn't set foot in the place. Anyway, she's too old. The hours would kill her. Besides, you don't want a woman in a gay bar." He made the bag stop bobbing and came to Dave. Taking away his empty glass, he looked into his eyes. "You know that." He headed for the kitchen.

"I know that." Dave went after him and leaned in the doorway. "Wendell's door was open. Johns and Mrs. Wendell at least agree on that. Leaving the fifteen hundred out of it for the moment, who could have gone there? Johns says he heard a voice arguing with Wendell. Whose voice was it?" Kegan dropped ice cubes. They ran away from each other across sleek yellow vinyl tiles. "Had Wendell had any fights with anyone? Tried to throw anybody out of The Hang Ten? Made enemies?"

"Enemies? Rick?" Kegan chuckled, tossing the ice cubes into the sink, opening the fridge for more. "If ever there was a guy you could say it about—that everybody loved him—it was Rick Wendell." He got two cubes safely into Dave's glass and poured bright new whiskey over them. "You be at that funeral. They'll be lined up around the block. He was a sweetheart." He handed Dave the glass.

Dave took it to the couch and sat there again. "Your sweetheart once," he said. "I saw the inscription on an old photo of you in his desk."

"Ancient history." Kegan bit into a shiny green apple and talked while he chewed. "Yeah, I was crazy about him. Crazy as I can be, for as long as I can

32

be. I'm a Libra with the moon in the seventh house."
He looked wanly toward the sunlit beach. "I can't
be what they used to call 'faithful.' I hated hurting
him, and believe me, nobody could look hurt the
way Rick could. I just couldn't do anything about
it. Wrong. I did what I could. I financed The Square
Circle. I was a good lightweight." Remembering, he
instinctively tightened his stomach muscles. "Well,
maybe not so good, but good-looking, you know
what I mean. They paid to watch me. And Rick
didn't have a dime. So I set up the bar and let him
run it for me. I made good bread in the fifties. They
televised fights a lot—remember? Bitched it was
ruining the fight game. Hell, it didn't hurt me." He
left-jabbed an imaginary opponent, and went into
the kitchen to get rid of the apple core. "No, if there
was anybody to throw out, I'd be the one to do that.
He hated confrontations."

"He was right," Dave said. "The last one was bad
for him." He drank again, lit a cigarette. "The fifteen
hundred dollars—if he didn't pay off the furniture
trucker, then it was in the envelope, right? Who else
could have known about it?"

"I told you." Kegan came, wiping apple juice off
his fingers onto his Levi's, to stand facing Dave. "I
didn't know about it myself."

"That's what you told me. And you also didn't
know Wendell had jumped the rails over a new boy.
You didn't even suspect it?"

"Second-guessing it, I should have." Kegan lifted
a foot and pushed with a brown toe at the crooked
stacks of magazines and records. "Soon as I

33

opened at noon, a phone call came, asking for him. Young-sounding. Wouldn't leave a name. But shit—that's not too unusual. Kids get it in their mind we're their buddies, you know? It's part of the business—everybody who buys a forty-cent beer is your friend. They choose one or the other of us. Usually Rick—he was so open about himself, easy talker."

He sighed and put a foot on the floor. "So—they get into scrapes or get depressed, they get on the phone. But when Rick came in at three-thirty, he said, yeah, he'd gotten the call at home. Then he phoned home and, the way it sounded, took up an argument he'd been having with Heather about her not getting out enough. He kept asking her to promise him she'd take in a flick that night, *The Sundown Studs.* She'd like the horses."

"She didn't like what they did to them," Dave said.

"But she went," Kegan said. "He really gave her a hard sell, argued with her for a half hour, telling her what a great movie it was. And I happened to know he'd never seen it. It only opened Friday. He hadn't got a night off to see it. Or an afternoon either. Not on a weekend." He frowned to himself, nodded. "Yeah, I should have figured out what he was up to." He gave Dave a bleak smile. "But frankly, Bobby was on my mind. That damn contest. On looks, he can win it going away. But a couple of dudes in that line-up have got a little intelligence, a lot of charm."

"When Wendell left early that night," Dave said, "that didn't add it all up for you—that there might be another Monkey in the picture?"

34

"No," Kegan said, "and I'll tell you why. It was Monday. Business was slow. We were just standing around. He said he might as well see the flick with her. It was natural."

Feet thudded on the deck outside. Bobby stood in the door opening. His long, blond muscles were slick with sweat. "Salad?" he panted. "Steak? I don't smell any charcoal."

Kegan looked at his watch. "It's not half an hour," he said. "Okay, okay. Go shower. It'll be ready when you get out." He watched the boy disappear down a dim white hallway, hopping, shedding the little shorts. Between the sun brown of his torso and legs, his butt gleamed white. Kegan sighed and started for the kitchen. "Steak for you?"

"Thanks but I've got to go," Dave said. "What about the Mr. Marvelous contest? How serious is it?"

"It's ridiculous." Kegan opened the refrigerator again. From beside the plastic flowers Dave watched him turn, arms loaded with lettuce, scallions, cucumbers, tomatoes, and dump them on a yellow Formica counter. "You mean, how serious do they take it?"

"You read me," Dave said.

"Well—it means a lot of free publicity for the bar that wins." Kegan found a paring knife in a drawer and sliced cucumbers. "That is, if they can keep the kid around for a few weeks, which isn't always easy. The kid himself wins clothes, cuff links, sporting goods, maybe a bicycle. You know, stuff put up by local merchants. It was mostly gay businesses at first. Now the straight ones ante up too."

He flashed Dave the sidelong wise grin again. "Pardon the word. And"—he brought a big yellow bowl out of a cupboard and started tearing lettuce leaves up and dropping them into it—"maybe a spot in a fuck film. Plus cash. Not much—whatever the participating taverns chip in. Last year it was maybe four, five hundred."

Dave said, "How stable are the kids?"

Kegan laughed. "They're hustlers, from anyplace, everyplace—dropouts, orphans, losers. Pathetic nobodies." He began work on the scallions with the paring knife. "Would-be movie actors who can't even memorize their own names, would-be rock stars who don't know a guitar from a frying pan."

From the end of the hall came the splash of a shower. Over the noise, Bobby sang in a cracked falsetto, "'Sunshine on my shoulders makes me happeee!'" Dave looked that way and said, "You know, Bobby is the same type as Johns—build, coloring, hair, mustache. Prettier, but the same type. Could somebody have it in for your entry?"

The knife rattled out of Kegan's fingers. He stared at Dave and he was pale under his tan. "Jesus," he breathed. "I never thought of that." His eyes narrowed. He drove a thick fist into a thick palm. "Yeah. What if one of those sick bastards decided they couldn't go up against Bobby? They could have tried to kill this Johns, thinking it was him, and got poor Rick by mistake. Christ—if Rick picked up Johns outside The Hang Ten and they drove off together . . ." Kegan looked sick. "Man, there's all kinds of animals around these days."

36

"And the other contestants would know Bobby?"

"Sure. Their pictures are in all the bar magazines." Wiping his hands on the Levi's again, he went past Dave to the coffee table and picked up a slender fold of coated stock. He flapped it open and pushed it into Dave's hand. Bobby was there with his unsure smile and not much else. So were eleven others. Kegan was right. None of them was as handsome as Bobby—unless the photos lied. Kegan said, "Take it along, if it'll help." He blinked up at Dave from under those swollen brow ridges. "You think there's really anything to it?"

At the hall's end, Bobby sang, "'Sunshine in my eyes can make me cry.'"

Dave folded the magazine into a side jacket pocket. "If I were you," he said, "I'd cancel the runs up the beach. Unless you run with him."

Ace was gazing unhappily down the hall. But he heard. "Yeah," he said faintly. "Thanks."

4

Seven draft beers and the glare of sunlight off windshields on freeways had given him a headache. He left the car under an old fig tree by someone's board back fence in a corner of the lot where he and Doug had leased spaces, and walked, tie loosened, jacket over arm, up Robertson past awninged shops where worm-eaten rocking horses, wicker dog baskets, brass bedsteads crowded the sidewalk, to a blue stucco building they'd rented that let Doug's gallery face the street and left the two of them big, ungainly sunlit rooms to echo around in upstairs.

The gallery doors were a pair, tall, carved, unvarnished and locked. He squinted at his watch. Only a quarter past four. He turned, lifted a tired hand to the portrait of himself, tall and alone in the Spanish arch window, and used a key on a blue door at the building's corner. It opened on narrow, straight stairs, the one feature of the place he disliked. As the door shut behind him and he started to climb, he heard voices. The acoustics in the hall were bad. There was loud rock music. He couldn't make out words.

When he reached the top of the stairs he went to where the voices were. Doug's room—skylight, easels, a paint-clotted zinc-top table with multiple shallow drawers for paints and brushes, blank canvases on stretchers leaning against a wall. Kovaks sat on the edge of an open bed, naked—pale urban skin, black stand-up hair, scraggly mustache. He leaned forward, elbows on knees, head hanging, a can of beer in one hand. Doug Sawyer, compact, dark-skinned, gray-haired, stood in the open doorway to a long roof deck where rubber trees rooted in plank boxes threw shadows on redwood garden chairs. Kovaks raised bloodshot eyes to Dave, gave him a crooked smile and said groggily:

"Hi, Dave."

Dave only looked at him and only looked at Doug when Doug turned to face him. Doug said, "He had lunch and fell asleep. I've been at my mother's." The beaky little woman kept a pet shop on a lost L.A. side street between a bicycle store and a beauty parlor. She'd begun having trouble with her mind lately—forgetfulness, delusions. The doctors said it had to do with poor circulation. Doug was having to spend more and more time looking after her.

Dave crouched and picked up a shallow bowl of thick bubbly amber glass from a scatter of ash on the floor beside the bed. In it lay the twisted butts of handmade cigarettes, burned down short. Dave held it out toward Doug. "Joints. I make it three."

"I'm coming down," Kovaks said sullenly, then giggled. "That's what the brew is for." He drank from the steamy can.

"I didn't ask you," Doug said. "You volunteered, remember? Gung ho. You were going to frame those

39

awful daubs for Mrs. What's-her-name." He walked
to a farther room and the rock racket did an audial
downcurve and quit. "I didn't expect that, but I did
expect you to be there."

"I was there from nine-thirty to one," Kovaks
said. "Then I got hungry. Yeah, I also felt like a low,
lazy high afterwards. Then I got sleepy. I was only
going to shut my eyes."

Doug leaned in a doorway and with a sad smile
shook his head at Dave. "He was spread out there
like smorgasbord."

"Come on," Kovaks said. "Kosher smorgasbord?"

"I want a shower," Dave said and passed Doug
in the doorway. Doug brushed his ear with a kiss.
"Whew! You smell like a brewery."

"I have been interviewing gay-bar owners," Dave
said. "It's a long, dull story. I'll tell you later." He
went on into his own room, which was the right
size and shape to play jai alai in, and began dropping his clothes, hearing Doug say to Kovaks:

"See these? Cards. Stuck in the door. Madge
Dunstan and Ray Lollard. Friends. Both of whom
would probably have bought something if the
gallery'd been open. They might even have bought
one of your pots."

"Forgive," Kovaks said in a broad and phony
Russian accent. "Kovaks bad. Do better next time.
He promise." The accent quit. "Oh, God," he
moaned, and metal crumpled. "The can's dry. Get
me another beer and I'll give you a kiss. Anyplace
you name."

Dave went into a big bathroom that was paved,

walled and domed in gaudy flowered Spanish tile. He took three aspirins, cranked the shower handles and stepped under the spray. He'd forgotten Ray Lollard after phoning him at noon from a sun-hot booth of salt crusty glass on Los Santos Pier. He'd gone to the pier, remembering how good the food used to be at a white wooden shack there called The Abalone. He hadn't reached Lollard—out to lunch. And The Abalone's management had changed. For the worse.

Sand dabs sautéed in butter and sprinkled with sesame seeds had been his favorite. These were uneatable, half cold, half raw. He made the best of the view, the good feel of the slow blue surf shaking the old pier stakes under the floorboards, and a cup of coffee, and laid open the bar magazine to study the addresses of the sponsors of entrants in the Mr. Marvelous contest. He made himself a mental map to follow. With some to-ing and fro-ing, he could hit seven on his way from Los Santos back to L.A. A fair start. He could get to the remainder tonight.

There'd been a sameness to them that was already blurring the places in his aching mind. Decor ranged from raw plywood (The Bunkhouse) to flocked crimson wallpaper (The Queen and Court). But the sad, aging patrons were interchangeable. So were the tunes on the jukeboxes. And so were the owners—around forty, too fleshy or too bony, in clothes too young and wigs styled sharply for last year—men long in the tooth and chatty. Dave had met five of the contestants too. All gathered at The Rawhide.

Kegan had been right. There was some charm, even some wit among them. The night Rick Wendell was murdered, this bunch had been together at a party in the Hollywood hills, celebrating the completion of a film in which they'd acted—if that was the word. Dave suspected it of being the same kind of film he'd rolled on Rick Wendell's bedside projector this morning. The sponsors of the other two boys said they'd been in the bars that evening, which, if it was true, narrowed down his list. He didn't regret that—not the way the bad beer and the worse bar air had left him feeling now.

He lathered, let the shower wash him down, first hot, then cold, and decided he'd live. He stepped out of the shower and Kovaks was standing at the toilet. Still naked. He pushed the flush handle, turned, looked Dave up and down. "You've got a nice body for a geriatric case."

"My heartfelt thanks," Dave said. "Excuse me." He reached past the lanky youth to get down a towel and walked out into the bedroom, using it. He heard, or maybe felt, Kovaks at his back and asked, "Where's Doug?"

"Down in the gallery." Kovaks blew on the back of Dave's neck and, chuckling softly, ran a hand along his shoulder, down his arm. "We won't be disturbed."

Dave pushed the towel at him. "You're already disturbed. Hang that up, please, then go get your clothes and drift back to your clay and wattles."

"There's a wattles shortage." Kovaks fell backward across Dave's bed and dropped the towel over his face. "Every wattles station in L.A. is closed. They paste up signs on the pumps—crooked, faltering, childlike lettering: 'Out of Wattles.' It's a conspiracy on the part of the big wattles producers to bring the American economy to its knees."

In the mirror over the chest where he was poking into drawers after underwear and socks, he saw Kovaks throw off the towel and sit up. His dark, long-lashed eyes went grave and pleading. He held out his hands. "Come on, Dave. Let's make it. I have this need."

Dave pulled on shorts. "It's all in your mind." Picking up the towel, he went back into the bathroom, rehung it and started brushing his teeth at the basin. In the doorway behind him, Kovaks said:

"It's a four-letter word for a part of the human anatomy but it's not m-i-n-d."

Dave spat peppermint suds, rolled his eyes up, said, "Aiee!" and rinsed his mouth. Pushing past Kovaks, he told him, "Try a cold shower." He went back to the chest for denims.

"I need a warm body," Kovaks said.

"Sorry." Dave kicked into the pants. "Only one to a customer." He zipped the pants, found his little book in the discarded suit jacket, sat on the bed and picked the phone up from the floor. There wasn't much furniture yet. He and Doug had moved in only six weeks ago and most of their time, energy and money had gone into fitting out the gallery. Up here, things were still bare. He dialed Ray Lollard again. A girl said:

43

"He left early, Mr. Brandstetter. I thought he was going to see you."

"He tried," Dave said. "I missed him. Thanks."

He hung up, pulled on a light jersey turtleneck, found Kovaks in Doug's room, seated on the bed again, in clay-stained dungarees, buckling warped sandals. He grumbled, "I feel like Bette Davis in *The Old Maid*."

"You'll never be an old maid," Dave said. "Not while the role of fifth wheel is open."

"I don't reject easy." Kovaks yanked a red-and-black-striped tank top over his flat torso. "I belong here somewhere. I know it. It's karma. If you—"

The street door opened below. A voice called, "Davey?" That had to be Madge Dunstan. She was Dave's oldest friend, a successful designer of textiles and wall coverings, a lean, handsome woman, sharp, tough-minded, good-humored. It always pleased Dave to see her. It pleased him something extra now because he'd had enough of Kovaks. And he didn't want to mishandle him. His pottery was exceptional and about the only thing bringing Doug any business yet. If Kovaks was to be dumped, it was up to Doug. Was Doug up to it?

Dave gave his head an impatient shake as he crossed the vast open space they'd decided was the living room. Two sets of shoes climbed the stairs. From the hall he looked down. Behind Madge, whose head was bent because she was watching her feet, came Ray Lollard, who smiled and said, "We met at Doug's fast-closed door and decided to bide our time over a drink across the street. You're back, just as I predicted. Both of you."

Kovaks stood by Dave. "All three," he said.

Madge's head came up. Lollard's eyebrows came up. And as they reached the stairhead, Dave told them, "This is Kovaks. He's trying to adopt us."

"Both of you?" Madge gave the bushy-haired youth her strong handshake and her best warm smile but the tilt of her head told Dave that Kovaks hadn't made a new friend. Not yet. "I thought," she said, "the *ménage à trois* went out with Noel Coward."

"It's back." Kovaks showed big white even teeth. "With ragtime piano and the John Held look."

"Kovaks," Lollard mused. "Then those would be your ceramics downstairs, no? Handsome. There's something so alive about them."

"I'm oversexed," Kovaks explained, and shook hands with Lollard.

"Maybe you'd better go turn down your kiln," Dave said, and took Lollard's elbow and began steering him back toward the kitchen. "Were you able to get me that name and address?"

Lollard moved reluctantly, looking back over his shoulder. "Aren't you lucky," he murmured enviously. "He's a dream."

"Of one kind or another," Dave said. "The name?"

"What? Oh. Yes. I'm sorry it took so long but it's new and unlisted." He handed Dave a slip of paper.

"Thomas Owens," Dave read aloud.

Kovak's flat soles were slapping down the stairs and Madge joined Dave and Lollard. "What about him?"

In a big old kitchen shiny with flowered tile, Dave began collecting gin, vermouth, pitcher, glasses, ice cubes. "I seem to know the name."

"Of course you do," Madge said. "You've met him at my house. More than once. An architect, remember? Nice guy. Until lately, too damn sad."

"How's that?" Dave made spiral cuts in a lemon rind. "He's the gaunt, kind of intense one with the yellow eyes, right? What was so sad? I forget that."

"We'd all given up on him," Lollard called. He stood at the front windows, peering down at the street, probably hoping for another glimpse of Kovaks. "Professionally, I mean."

Madge said, "He kept getting commissions, then losing them by insisting things would be done either his way or not at all."

"That can keep an architect poor, yes." Dave loosened ice cubes from a tray and dumped them into the pitcher, which had been living in the freezer and was coated with snow. "It's not the freest of the seven deadly arts, is architecture."

"It's curious too," Madge said. "He's so sweet and giving, so gentle and kind personally. I guess a word might be *yielding*. Everybody loves him. Even other architects. And I don't mean just respect. They've got that too, but tenderness, a kind of sheltering attitude, protective. Everybody wants to help him. That's the mystifying part. Nobody could."

Dave began turning the ice with a glass rod. "Did he ever bring a Larry Johns to your house? Maybe twenty, twenty-one, blond, about five eleven, hundred fifty pounds, long yellow hair and mustache?"

"He never brought anyone." Madge wandered into the hall and out onto the roof garden. Her words drifted in through the open kitchen window. "He lives with a widowed sister he supports, has for years. But she has a child and they never came. I suspect she'd be uncomfortable in a room not filled with reliably heterosexual matrons. Anyway, his fortunes have changed at last. He's built some stunning beach houses."

Lollard came the long walk back across the living room. "For film people," he said, "show business people. He finally found one too busy with road shows or Las Vegas or something to bother him. What he built was marvelous. After that, everyone wanted one."

"He just lately finished a lovely place for himself, only a couple of miles from me," Madge called. "What's the name of this big, climbing thing with the perforated leaves. *Monstera* something, right?"

"*Deliciosa*," Dave said. "Do you know anybody in the bar, restaurant, hotel supply business, Madge?"

"Any number." Madge came back in with a kite-size green leaf in her hand. She leaned against the refrigerator, holding it up, studying it. "What's on your mind? Yes, this place is big and empty, but surely—"

"No, no." Dave put a glass into the bony, freckled hand that wasn't busy with the leaf. "What I need to know is if you've heard of any ripoffs lately, like a truckload of padded leather chairs on swivels."

Madge had taken a mouthful of martini. She shook her head and swallowed. "That was last year. A renegade truckdriver sold it for his own profit instead of delivering it where it had been ordered."

"Good." Dave put a glass into Ray Lollard's hand. He asked Madge, "Do you remember who bought it?"

"Well, now, but wait." She frowned. "It wasn't chairs. It was high stools, the big, deep, cushiony kind. Yes—a gay bar in Surf. What's it called? They were remodeling, raising the bar, putting in walnut paneling, padding everything in leather. Naturally, when the police came around, they gave the stools back. They hadn't known they were stolen."

"The Hang Ten?" Dave asked.

She nodded quickly. "That's the one."

48

5

It lay in the dunes like elegant wreckage. Nearing, he saw that the crazily angled upthrusts of varnished boards were walls and roofs. When he topped the last dune, clumped grasses snagging his pants legs, what had looked to be broken and strewn by accident shaped into a structure. Under wooden wedges of overhang, triangles of smoke-dark glass drank light. The same kind of glass in very tall panes, sill to roof beam, mirrored surf, sky, horizon. A deck of gapped and biased planking reached high out over jagged rocks. Blankness watched from towers bleak as prairie storefronts.

When he climbed wide, shallow board steps, dogs barked indoors. They were assorted. Two small ones clawed the dark panes of a broad wood-frame door. One was slick-haired, pumpkin-colored, with a curled tail. He jumped like a dwarf acrobat. The other bared fierce little fangs. He was ruffed. Behind them, a big one stood square and solemn and barked basso. He was marked like a German shepherd but was lop-eared.

A girl came among them. She wore sunglasses. Her mouth was darkly bruised and swollen. She'd parted her taffy-color hair in the middle and tied it back. The man's shirt she wore had random appliqués of peasanty flowers. Its tails hung out over gray bell bottoms. Her feet were bare. She smiled at Dave. Startlingly, her two upper front teeth were missing. In mock despair at the racket of the dogs, she put her hands over her ears. Then she waved them at the big dog, who backed off, looking hurt. She grabbed the collar of the slick little one, the harness of the ruffed one, and dragged them, cringing, over a sleek floor into a place out of Dave's sight, where they stopped barking. When she came back and opened the door she was panting a little and bright pink was in her cheeks. "What can I do for you?"

"I'm Brandstetter. I phoned yesterday, remember? To talk to Tom Owens. That didn't work out. I thought I might have better luck in person. Will you tell him I'm here? He'll remember me. We met at Madge Dunstan's."

"Oh?" She made her mouth small, half apologetic, half resentful. "You didn't say that on the phone."

"I didn't have his name at the time," Dave said. "Only his number. Can I see him?"

"Well . . ." Her forehead puckered. She glanced over her shoulder. "He's got somebody with him now. Vern Something. An old school buddy." Her mouth turned down. "They act like they never graduated. People don't get old, do they? On the inside, I mean. They're, like, sixteen all their lives."

"We try to keep it secret," he said. "I'll wait." He stepped toward her. She wasn't as good at blocking off a door as she was at blocking off a phone. She stepped back. "Well—okay."

The room he came into was long and lofty and full of sea light. Raw wicker furniture with sailcloth cushions was grouped around a black cowl fireplace in a corner. A long wicker couch with a long, low deal table in front of it looked at the beach. A fastness of glossy plank floorboards was islanded by Navajo rugs, big ones and good. They were bringing scary prices now. He knew. In the shop full of silver and turquoise and Polynesian feathered masks under the old L.A. Museum, he and Doug had priced rugs like these. Priced them and given up.

The girl went away noiselessly. Dave counted sailboats tilting between the beach and hulking offshore oil-drilling platforms misted by distance. Wood creaked above and behind him and he turned. A tremendous painting that might have been gulls in a storm or simply slashes of white on ultramarine went along the room's back wall under a gallery. A youth of maybe twenty came along the gallery. Sun had turned him dark brown. A helmet of black hair covered his ears. He wore a tie-dyed shirt in faded yellows and oranges, sleeves torn off at the armholes, baggy surfer trunks. A leather case on a shoulder strap jounced at his hip when he came down stairs that were like a flight of wooden birds.

"Trudy!" he called and saw Dave and stopped, turned his head slightly, mistrustful. "Who are you?"

"Brandstetter," Dave said.

"It's about Larry, isn't it?" the boy said.

"Yes. Who are you?"

The boy laughed without humor. "She thought nobody would find out. I told her they would. A murder. They're going to find out because they're going to try. Tom knew it. But not Gail, not Gail."

"They're not trying," Dave said. "I'm trying. They're willing to settle for Johns. I'm not."

The boy squinted disbelief. "Not a private eye. They don't really have those, do they? Cannon? Barnaby Jones? All that fantasy shit on the schlock box?" His laugh was loud and forced. His eyes were watchful.

"Not so far as I know," Dave said. "I work for an insurance company. Money, not fantasy. You live here? You know Larry Johns?"

"I'm here for the summer. Trudy's guest. From college. Yeah, I know him. Tom kept sending Trudy drawings and stuff of the house. He never mentioned Larry. I'd have used my plane ticket, only it's got a forty-day stipulation on it."

"You didn't like him?"

The boy worked his mouth as if he'd tasted something rotten. "Did you like *Midnight Cowboy?* I didn't."

Dave cocked an eyebrow. "Was that how you saw him?"

"That's what he was. Only in the movie, the dude wasn't any good at peddling his ass. Larry made out." The boy's glance measured the soaring room. "Look where he landed."

"He landed in trouble," Dave said. "The worst kind. Why did you want to use your plane ticket? This is a big place. Did you have to trip over him?"

"I didn't," the boy said sourly. "Trudy did. Sickening. A Texas redneck." He creased a square

52

forehead above thick black brows. "What have they got, for God sake? I mean, they're dominating the stupid culture, all of a sudden. Seriously—everything's country western now. Have you noticed? Even politics. Washington's wall-to-wall fatback and collard greens. That nauseating down-home twang. Even reporters. It's like all the TV sets were made in Amarillo, or something. His old man worked in the oil fields, could barely write his name. He bragged about it."

"You wouldn't be jealous?" Dave asked.

He narrowed his eyes, flared his nostrils, showed his teeth. "'Brown eyes,'" he hissed, "'say, *love me, or I keel you.*'" He dropped the act. "No. I told her what he was. A hustler. Taking her uncle for all he could get. Didn't faze her. She felt *sorry* for him."

From somewhere beyond wooden bulkheads she called, "Mr. Brandstetter?" Dave took steps, craned to see. She stood by a distant doorway, Vermeer light pouring over her. "Excuse me," he said and went there. The boy came after him, bare heels thumping.

The light came through a tall gap in the wall above the door. The room beyond the door held a high hospital bed but it was meant for an office, a workroom. Drafting table. T squares, straight-edges, triangles. Plywood bins out of which poked rolled blueprints, floor plans, elevations. Half-empty shelving. Tall stools from an unfinished-furniture shop, price tags still hanging off rungs. Roof windows funneled down north light. Low in a corner, a window framed surf breaking on jagged rocks. The tunnel you looked out into was the sun-ribbed shadow of the deck above.

Tom Owens lay in the bed. About thirty-five, long-boned, with long pale-red hair, long pale-red mustache. Yellow wasn't the accurate word for his eyes. Tawny would probably do it. A bolted frame-work on the bed foot was strung with weights and pulleys to keep his legs raised. The legs were in bulky plaster casts. The bed was strewn with maga-zines, paperback books. A man stood at its far side. Chinos, T-shirt, thin red windbreaker jacket—boyish, all new. He was laughing. But sad was the impres-sion he gave. He could have been younger than Owens but life had used him harder. Owens had been smiling at whatever he'd said. Then he turned his head on the pillows, saw Dave and lost the smile. But he held out his hand.

"Dave Brandstetter. After your call yesterday, I remembered you."

Dave shook the hand. "We met at Madge Dunstan's."

"How is Madge?" Owens picked up a cigarette pack from a folded newspaper. The Los Santos *Tide*. RITES FOR MURDERED TAVERN OWNER. "You've met my niece, Trudy?" He lit a cigarette. "And Mark Dimond? Her"—he blinked amused bafflement at her—"do they still say 'fiancé'?"

Trudy shook her head. "'Lover,'" she said.

"'Old man,'" Mark Dimond said.

"Right!" Trudy laughed and kissed his nose. She looked at her uncle. "Are you okay? Can I get you anything? I don't know why Mother's not back.

We want to go tape sea gulls and waves and like that."

"Go." Owens smiled. "I'm fine."

They went. "We'll take the dogs," Trudy called back, and Mark Dimond groaned.

Dave said, "Madge is all right but what happened to you?"

"I leaned on the rail of the deck." He jerked his head up to show which deck he meant. "It wasn't bolted in place. Temporary nails holding it. A detail Elmo Sands overlooked. My contractor. I wouldn't have believed it. He doesn't forget anything. Ever. But—the rail gave and I landed on those rocks. Not gracefully."

Dave winced and the man on the far side of the bed said, "Listen, Tommy, I better split." He looked at Dave with soft, long-lashed child eyes. "You've got more important things to do."

"Vern"—Owens reached out, gave the man's arm a squeeze—"it's been good. Dave Brandstetter, Vern Taylor. Vern's just turned up after seventeen years. How about that?" Owens's eyes smiled at the man. Gently affectionate. As at a backward child.

"We were in high school together. West L.A." Taylor came around the bed to shake Dave's hand. "Lived on the same tacky street. Both our dads sold appliances at Sears." He looked Dave up and down. It gave Dave the feel of being wistfully priced, like candy behind glass. Taylor smiled a sixth-birthday smile that was marred by bad silver dentistry. "Now he's a big-time architect. Is that what you are too?"

"Insurance," Dave said. "Claims investigator."

Something happened to Taylor's smile. He said guardedly, "Oh? Yeah?" He worked up his euphoria again. "Well, it must seem crazy to a stranger but I'm really excited. Nobody else in our class turned out to amount to a damn. Me especially." His laugh didn't even try for irony. "I've got failure down to a system. Like my dad. But look at this." He lifted his hands and let them fall. "Just look at it! Isn't it great? Last time I saw him, he was stumbling over hurdles in gym, just like the rest of us. And where do I see him next? On a big TV talk show. Magazine color spreads—beach homes for movie stars, swanky town-house condominiums. He's a celebrity." He grabbed Owens's hand and shook it hard. "Listen, Tommy—I'll come back. But you're busy. I mean, important people. What time have you got for nobodies like Vern Taylor?" At the room door he turned back. He pleaded, "We had some laughs, though, didn't we? Talking over old times?"

"It was a good morning," Owens said. "Do it again."

"Get better, now." Taylor lifted a hand, went away.

Owens told Dave, "Sit down." His voice was heavy. Dave put himself in one of a pair of new director's chairs—orange canvas, varnished pine. Owens said, "So now you've found out where he lived. Does it matter? Does it have to matter? He wanted to keep it secret."

"Wanted to and did," Dave said. "Why?"

"To protect me," Owens said. "You've probably got an opinion about Larry. Everybody has. The same one. A hustler. No morals. Well, it's not so."

56

"What was he doing in Rick Wendell's bed?"

Red flared in the taut skin across Owens's cheekbones. "That's not what I'm talking about. I don't know but I know he would have explained it."

"And you'd have accepted what he said?" Dave asked. "A nice arrangement. For him."

"I meant he wouldn't kill anybody. He didn't have it in him."

"Why did he go with Wendell?" Dave glanced around. "I've seen the Wendell place. Johns was better off here. You kept him, right?"

Owens said defensively, "He'd never had a family. Father deserted his mother when he was born. Mother put him in a home, then vanished. He got passed from hand to hand until he was old enough to go out on his own. No education to speak of, no opportunities. I wanted to turn things around for him."

Dave said, "Every hustler on Hollywood Boulevard tells that story."

"Maybe it's true." Owens was combative. "Maybe that's why they're on Hollywood Boulevard."

Dave grunted, leaned forward, held out his cigarette pack. "Was Wendell a friend of his? Or did he just get lonely for the life, walk out on the highway, stick out his thumb? And Wendell stopped. He was supposedly on his way to see a film with his mother."

"I don't know." Owens had taken a cigarette. He rolled it in long, knuckly fingers, watching it grimly. "If you think I've been able to sleep for wondering, you're wrong." Dave clicked a slim steel lighter and Owens hung the cigarette in his mouth and turned his head against the pillows for the flame. "Thanks. Maybe the coffee in that thing is still hot." On a pivot table next to the bed pottery mugs waited beside a stout plastic vessel with a handle. Dave went to it, turned the screw top, poured into two mugs, screwed the top back. Owens worked a button on the bed frame that set a small motor humming and got him into a more upright position. Dave handed him a mug. Owens said, "Wendell owned a gay bar. Larry might have known him."

"The Hang Ten," Dave said. "Were you ever there?"

"No. I've seen the sign. On the beach in Surf."

"That's it. Did Johns ever mention it?"

"Not that I remember." Owens sipped at the coffee, tightened his mouth, shook his head. "Larry was vague about a lot of things. Including how long he'd been on the scene here. I didn't pry, I didn't care. I was too happy to have found him."

"Let me guess," Dave said. "He was the first."

"There were baths, back seats of cars, cheap motels. When it got unbearable." Owens laughed sadly without sound. "But yes, the first at home. We were in pretty close quarters, Gail and Trudy and I." He looked at the spacious room. "It seems like a bad dream, remembering. The way we used to live. Mostly on unemployment. I'd get a drafts-man's job. Government projects—county, state, schools, hospitals. I'd last till some so-called architect handed me something too stupid. I wouldn't say anything. That's not my style. I'd just walk out and hunt another job. Nights, I kept designing stuff on my own." He gave a shamed shrug. "Sure, I dreamed of a Larry Johns but it wasn't rational. I hadn't the time. To say nothing of money. I had a family to look after."

"You raised Trudy?" Dave said. "That was kind."

Owens brushed the words aside. "It was the way things worked out. She was four when her father died in Korea. Not in the war. Afterward—the occupation. Jeep accident. His lieutenant's pension wasn't big enough for the two of them to live on. Gail would have had to work. She had no skills. Anyway, there was no one to leave the baby with."

"Then she wasn't a baby anymore," Dave said, "and you had time. And money. And privacy. So there was a Larry Johns, right? Where did you find him?"

Owens flushed again, looked away, mumbled, "Hitching a ride at a freeway on-ramp. I'd been to an AIA dinner. I was smashed." He looked back. "In the morning it would figure I'd be sorry, wouldn't it? I wasn't."

"Are you sorry now?" Dave asked. "You didn't exactly jump to help him."

"I picked up the phone when I saw the eight A.M. news Tuesday." He eyed a neat television set on one of the empty shelves. "Gail grabbed the phone and set it out of reach. Just as she hung up on you yesterday. She's always known what was best for me." He grimaced. "I've let her get away with it too long. Over the years it's become a habit. A bad one. For both of us."

"She's trying to protect you," Dave said. "You respect that in Johns."

The yellow eyes blinked. "Okay—touché. You're right. She loves me. In her she-bear way."

"You were going to phone a lawyer?" Dave asked.

Owens nodded. "All Gail could see was that I'd be smeared. Scandal. Homosexuality. Murder. I didn't care. I love him. He loves me."

Dave said, "He went to Wendell."

"But he loves me." Owens was stubborn. "The way he kept my name out of it proves that. And day by day— There are things you can't fake."

"That depends who's watching." Dave turned to the window, drank from the mug. Trudy crouched over the tape deck on the rocks while the dogs wagged around her and Dimond stood in the swirling surf holding a microphone. "Where did he tell you he was going that night?"

"He didn't. I'd taken pills." He nodded at his casts. "The itching can drive you crazy. When I woke, he wasn't with me. Wasn't in the house at all. Trudy was home. I had her look for him."

"What happened to Trudy's face?"

"She smashed up her mother's car. A Vega, less than six months old, never given a bit of trouble. Then—the brakes failed. She and Mark were up the canyon, headed for a rock festival. Totaled the car but they got off. He cracked some ribs, she lost those teeth, blacked her eyes. But considering—"

Dave frowned. "When was this?"

"Week ago Sunday. Two days later, I fell." Owens finished off his coffee. "I'd had a lot of luck. Suddenly it reversed itself. Still—I'm alive, the kids are alive. Gail might have been driving. She's alive.

60

Sequoia Insurance paid up without any questions. We're all right. Then came this thing about Larry. They say bad luck runs in threes. I'm hoping it's over."

"Not for him," Dave said. "It's only started. The police and the district attorney don't share your blind faith. They want him locked up forever."

"And you?" Owens studied him. "What do you want?"

"To find out what really happened. No insurance company likes a murder. Not with so much wrong with it. For instance, did Johns need fifteen hundred dollars?"

Owens was stubbing out his cigarette in a brown pottery ashtray on a stack of magazines. His head jerked up. "The news reports didn't mention robbery."

"And he hadn't asked you for money?"

"Not then or ever," Owens said. "Which makes him a pretty strange kind of hustler, doesn't it?" He gave a short laugh, then frowned. "What would he want with fifteen hundred dollars?"

"I don't know and he didn't get it." Dave bent to put out his cigarette. "But Wendell had drawn it from his bank on his way to work and the empty envelope was on his desk at home and I've been lied to about what the money was for." Reminded of Ace Kegan, he read his watch, gave Owens his hand to shake. "I've got to go. I'm sorry if this has been tiring."

Owens kept hold of the hand for a moment. "You can help him, can't you? Madge says you're tops in your field. You find answers when the police don't."

"Only if the answers are there." Dave went to the door with the upreach of open wall above it. Hand on the knob, he turned. "Is he stable? Emotionally? Does he have hangups?"

"You mean, would he have gone out of his head and killed Wendell for making a pass at him? No. He's easy and uncomplicated. There was a catch phrase a while back that sums up his attitude pretty accurately: 'If it feels good, do it.'"

"That couldn't include killing people?" Dave said.

"No way," Owens said.

Joseph Hansen

6

The car was a ten-year-old mini—Swedish, French, Italian? The color of dried blood. It stood by the guardrail, a broad steel band bolted to squat posts that divided road shoulder from beach. At the rear of the car a leaf-shaped flap of slatted steel was raised, showing a dirty little motor. Vern Taylor stood staring at it, sea wind flapping his flimsy red jacket. Dave pulled his car onto the gravel and got out. Taylor frowned at him, then smiled.

"Oh, hi. Thanks for stopping. I'm not sure just what's wrong. It suddenly quit." Gulls wheeled screaming overhead. He looked at them as if it were their fault. "Hell, I only bought it a couple weeks ago." His half smile was shamefaced. "No, it didn't cost much. But you'd think it ought to stagger along for a month."

"Just long enough for the dealer to move to another lot and change names." Dave leaned to look at the works. "You've tried everything?"

"I worked in garages for a while but I don't know everything." Taylor had given up. He gave the empty sky a look, the empty hills, the empty sea. "Way out here. Listen, can you give me a lift? Into Surf?"

"No problem." Dave slammed down the tinny

engine cover, led the way to the Electra glistening silver in the sun, opened the passenger door, walked around and slid behind the wheel. Taylor got in gingerly, as if afraid he'd soil the new upholstery. He shut the door with soft caution and sat rigid like a child in church. Dave pulled the car back into the coast-road traffic.

"Nice car," Taylor said. "There's a lot of money in insurance, isn't there? I read that somewhere. Richest corporations in the country."

"My father's the corporation," Dave said. "I'm only an employee. It's a company car."

"Medallion," Taylor said. "That's that tall glass-and-steel tower on Wilshire. Beautiful. You know what my father did?"

"Sold appliances at Sears," Dave said.

"Right. I read someplace that if your father was a success, you'd be a success too."

"He worked hard for it," Dave said.

"I guess you'll get it all when he dies." Taylor found a crumpled cigarette in the red jacket and lit it with a paper match. "When my dad died, you know what I got? I got to pay all his bills. I'd made out a little better than he did. No wife and kids to support. I made a liar out of that book. For a while, anyway. Of course, that was quite a while ago." He was holding the burned match. Dave tilted open the ashtray under the dash. Taylor put the match into it carefully. "I was in architecture too, you know? Well, contracting, really. Draftsman. Tom and I took drafting together. Sat right next to each other. Anyway, I had enough to pay what my dad left owing. Then. If he died today, I don't know what I'd do. I'm no draftsman anymore."

"What do you do?" Dave asked.

"Wash dishes," Taylor answered in a thin voice. But when Dave glanced at him, he was smiling. Hard. Like a brave little kid with a skinned knee. "At the marina. They've got a lot of fancy restaurants there. I mean, what I do, really, is load up these big machines. They do the washing. But what they call you is still a dishwasher. I'll bet Tom eats where I wash dishes. How about that for a joke? His dad worked at Sears too. Lived in the same kind of crummy little house right up the block from us."

"He won't be eating in restaurants for a while," Dave said.

"Oh, you mean his legs. Was that why you were there today? Looking into the accident? Boy, that was really careless of that contractor. Imagine—a beautiful house like that. A hundred thousand dollars, I'll bet. And he couldn't even bolt the porch rail."

"It could have been worse," Dave said. "Owens could have been killed."

"I don't think so," Taylor said.

Dave glanced at him again, brows lifted.

"Seriously. I read in some book how if you've got a lot of money, you rarely have fatal accidents. Or illnesses. Unless you're old, of course. And they don't even age as fast as other people. Isn't that interesting? I mean, there are statistics about it, charts. There's magic in money. It's the magic of our acquisitive society. Protects you from all evil. Nothing can get the better of money. Suppose Tom killed someone."

Dave squinted. "You think he killed someone?"

"No, no. But I mean, what if he did? He'd get off. People like that can hire expensive lawyers and they know how to delay and delay, and appeal and appeal. They can go right up to the Supreme Court if they have to, you know? And if they still said he was guilty, all he'd get would be a light sentence. He'd be out in a few months, maybe. Poor, you're jailed for months even before your trial can come up." Suddenly he wasn't chattering like a wound-up kid. He sounded bitter. "And then they really nail you."

At a traffic halt where, on the right, the charred stakes of a collapsed and burned-out amusement pier stuck up through the flat blue slide of surf, Dave swung the Electra left onto Jetty Street. At the corner a chili stand raised a make-believe lighthouse, plaster scaling off it, grimy windows red-framed at the top. In lots with rusty chain-link fences, forgotten boat hulls reared up on scaffolds deep in weeds. Auto junkyards shouldered vacant store buildings. Tiller wheels cracked and warped in the fretwork of cottage porches. "Maybe you should read another book," Dave said.

"Oh?" Taylor pulled a little dime-store notebook from a hip pocket and began patting his jacket for something to write with. "What's the title?"

"Any title," Dave said. "Just a different book."

Taylor put the note pad away. "You don't agree? No. You're rich yourself. I mean, psychologically, that would be natural. Just like it's natural for me to believe what the book said. Because I'm poor."

"Where do you want me to drop you?" Dave said.

"Oh, turn at the next stop. Cortez. Right. It's down in the middle of the block." On a bleak, sunlit corner, black women in bright headcloths waited in a skirmish of small children outside a brick store building where a cardboard window sign said FOOD STAMPS. Taylor's arm came up stiff. "There." The building he pointed at was square-cornered, pale-brown shiplap, three stories. Rickety outdoor stairs climbed the side and faded lettering crossed a high false front. SEA-VIEW ROOMS WEEKLY RATES. Dave pulled to the curb.

"It's a lie." Taylor used his silver-filled little-boy smile. "You can't see a square inch of ocean. Not from my room, for sure. The cheap ones are at the back. What I see is oil wells. But it's great being at the beach. I always lived in L.A. before. Listen, thank you very much for the ride. You really rescued me. I hope I didn't take you too far out of your way. It's really nice to have met you." He put out a hand for Dave to shake. "You're the only new friend of Tom's I've met. And you're just what I expected."

"Yup," Dave said. "I wear three-hundred-dollar suits and drive an eight-thousand-dollar car. Mr. Taylor—stop measuring people that way."

"It's American," Taylor said defensively.

"And Nigerian. And Bolivian," Dave said. "It started in Sumer."

"Don't misunderstand me,"Taylor said. "I'm glad about Tom's success. I mean, we started out life together. We were close." His soft brown eyes looked into Dave's. Too steadily. "Very, very close. One summer, especially." A flush darkened the time-etched skin of his cheekbones. "You understand what I'm saying."

Dave edged him a smile.

"Sure you do. I knew you would. So you can understand how happy it makes me that one of us got someplace in life. It's the truth. I couldn't be happier if it had happened to me."

"Right." Dave pushed his cuff back.

Taylor read the gesture and fumbled the car door open. "You have to go. You're busy. When people get in your income bracket, they work all the time. Anybody who thinks money lets you take it easy is an idiot. I read. I know." He got out, eased the door shut, crouched so the window framed his used boy face, the wind fluttering his soft hair. "I guess you'll be talking to that contractor now, about that deck rail."

"Not now," Dave said, "but sooner or later."

"He'll blame it on some workman," Taylor said. "The poor bastard will get fired."

"What about your car?" Dave asked.

Taylor looked doubtful. "I'll figure out something. Have to have a car. Gosh, I have an important appointment today too." He used the ragged smile again. "Besides, I have to get around, catch up on things. Did you know, they've got movies now where they show everything?" His leer was prepubic. "And boys dancing naked in the bars? They call them go-go boys. The bars are having a contest for the most beautiful boy." He patted the window ledge, stood. "Don't want to miss that." He turned away. "And my friends," he said dreamily. "I have to see my friends."

Wind had strung Bobby's long yellow hair across his face. He lay asleep in the small white trunks on a big towel printed with gaudy flowers. The beach was crowded—surfers, girls in next to nothing, babies in nothing, dogs. But even from the distance of Ace Kegan's deck—no one home in the apartment behind it—Dave had picked the boy out easily. He shone. Dave waded through a wash of guitar discords and bongo drums and sat down next to the towel. He took off a shoe, emptied sand out of it, put it back on. Into Bobby's ear, a battery radio sang in a bright bad-ass voice about soft drinks. Dave tied the shoe and asked: "Didn't Ace tell you it's risky to be out here alone?"

The boy didn't open his eyes. His beautiful mouth muttered, "Not alone. Five thousand people."

"Where's Ace?" Dave emptied the other shoe. "I want to ask him a question."

"He's talking to some lawyer." Bobby used his fingers to rake the hair off his face. He pushed himself up on his elbows, squinting against the brightness of the sky. "Something wrong?"

"Probably." Dave put the shoe back on and tied it. "Unless it's about remodeling he's seeing that lawyer?"

69

"What?" Bobby's face twisted. He switched off the radio. "Remodeling? The Hang Ten?"

"That's what he told me," Dave said.

"You must have heard him wrong. They remodeled last year. Did it all over in leather." On the towel lay an empty soft drink can, Kleenex in a little box printed with antique cars, a brown squeeze bottle of suntan lotion, a pack of Marlboros. Bobby groped among them for sunglasses, hooked them on. Polaroids. They mirrored Dave in silver. "Why would they remodel it already? It cost a bundle and it still looks like new."

"Right." Dave picked up the books, shuffled them. *30 Days to a More Powerful Vocabulary. Contemporary American Poetry. A Zen Primer. The Best and the Brightest.* "At a guess, you're supposed to be studying."

"Yeah, well, Christ. I'm tired. I was in that God damn bar till two." Now he probed a cigarette from his pack and worked at lighting paper matches the sea wind blew out. "You know, Ace is great on working you. All energy, you know? He really can't figure somebody it doesn't mean the world to to win that stupid contest."

Dave brought out his lighter, cupped the flame, held it till Bobby got the light. "It's for your own good," he said.

"Shee-it." Bobby turned onto his belly, rested his chin on folded arms. The smoke blew away from his mouth along the sand. "Anyway, he doesn't see I can't do three things at once. He wants a bartender, a college student and a body-building freak all in one."

Dave set the books down. "You tend bar much?"

"Ace is nervous, runs around like a white rat in one of those labs. He'll phone anytime and say, 'Get your ass over here.'"

Dave watched surfers crest a long blue swell and vanish in a kick and flail of arms and legs. He said very carefully, "Like Monday?"

"Yeah, for instance," Bobby said. "All of a sudden, about eight. I mean, he's stacked up operas and symphonies for me to listen to, half a library to read. Not just read, man—memorize, you know? Then he calls and I've got to take over The Hang Ten for the night." He turned onto his back again, onto his elbows. "And at seven the next morning he starts asking questions with my boiled eggs. Big treat, two days a week—boiled eggs. Quizzing me on the music, on the books. How could I read the fucking books? I was working. You slop beer for a hundred faggots all by yourself sometime—you'll know what work is."

"I'll bet," Dave said. "Did he tell you why he had to go out?"

"Wait a minute." Bobby sat up. "That was the night Rick was killed." He poked the cigarette into the sand. "Who are you?" He pulled off the sunglasses. "Some kind of cop?" He got to his knees. "Yeah. What else is new? Shit!" He punched the sand with a fist. He looked ready to cry. "Now I've got him in trouble."

"He was already there." Dave stood up, brushed sand off his suit. "That's probably why he's seeing that lawyer."

"It's about the partnership," Bobby said loudly. "There's a lot to straighten out, now Rick's dead."

Dave said, "When did he come back to the bar on Monday night?"

"He didn't. He was home when I got there. Passed out, if you want to know. He'd killed half a fifth of Canadian Club." His eyes came up suddenly, scared.

"He doesn't drink," Dave said.

"That's why he passed out," Bobby said. "Look— what do you want? To stick him for Rick's murder?"

"No. That's up to the police," Dave said. "But I'm uneasy about their present choice. It doesn't make sense. What do you think? You know Ace. Could he have murdered Rick Wendell?"

"Listen." Bobby was shaking and under the saffron mustache his mouth was a bad color. "Get away from me. Will you? Please? Just get away from me."

"Easy," Dave said. "I'm not a cop. And I can't hurt anybody. Not you. Not Ace. It doesn't work that way, Bobby. People hurt themselves. Sometimes their friends can turn that around. Like possibly now."

Bobby said sulkily, "He's got a lousy temper." He hooked the glasses on again, knelt, gathered up his traps. "Now leave me alone, will you? I don't want to talk to you—all right?" He walked off, dragging the flowered towel. Dave went after him.

"A bad enough temper to shoot somebody?"

"No. Fists are all he knows. He hits people. He's been in court about it." Bobby lengthened his stride toward the apartment deck, where the chrome-plated stem of the punching bag glittered. Dave kept pace.

"Rick had a new lover. Wasn't Ace worried?"

"What?" Bobby turned sharply. The radio fell. A lanky brown dog came from under a faded beach umbrella and sniffed at it. Was it a lunch box? Bobby kicked at the dog and picked up the radio. The dog slunk back to the umbrella, where a mound of old white flesh slept in gingham ruffles. "He never mentioned it. Anyway, he wouldn't hurt Rick. Hell, he was always protecting the big, dumb slob. They were friends. A long time."

"Till death did them part," Dave said.

"Yeah," Bobby said. "Get lost, will you?"

Two miles up the beach from Ace Kegan's, on battered benches in the sun, along a gritty walk that marked off Surf's crumbling ocean-front apartment houses and dim stores from the beach, old men argued with each other in loud Yiddish. Long-haired, bearded boys played guitars and tambourines and grinned while a bowlegged little old woman with a Day-Glo kerchief over her hair did a slow Polish village dance. A pack of breedless dogs ran past, tongues lolling.

The Hang Ten turned a blank stucco face to the scene. Bolted to its door was a wooden surfer, clumsily chiseled in low relief. Wind had piled trash at his feet, greasy burrito wrappers, Big Mac boxes, Styrofoam cups. These crunched under Dave's shoes as he put on his glasses to read a yellowed card tacked at the edge of the door. In faded felt-pen lettering, the bar's hours showed. 12 NOON—2 A.M. He checked his watch. Noon had passed but the door's three padlocks were clamped.

He found a phone booth and dialed his office. For messages. There'd been half a dozen calls. His secretary told him about them in a thin whimper. A terrified skinny little girl of sixty, Miss Taney had teetered on the edge of nervous collapse all her life. The names of three of the callers meant nothing to Dave. The fourth had been Lieutenant Yoshiba of the Los Santos police, upset about something. The fifth had been Heather Wendell, upset about something. The sixth had been Gail Ewing, Tom Owens's sister—upset about something.

Yoshiba was out to lunch. At the Wendell house it was the gaunt giant Billy who picked up the receiver. The lost husband and father. Found. Dave estimated it was the phone in his son's rooms he was using. That would put him near the bottles. He sounded as if he'd had one in his hand for a few hours. One or more. He tried to work up indignation. Why didn't Dave leave his wife alone? Wasn't it bad enough to have lost her son? What did Dave mean, telling Ace Kegan he thought she'd killed Rick? He, Billy, had heard Ace say it at the funeral. Where was Heather? At a lawyer's office, that's where.

"I'll get back to her," Dave said.

"You're in trouble," Billy warned him.

"I've got a lot of company," Dave said.

The dogs barked into the phone again at Tom Owens's beautiful beached ark. Gail Ewing said, "I'm extremely unhappy with you for disturbing

Tom. He had nothing to do with this horrible business. It was poor judgment on his part to take that boy in. Obviously. But that doesn't mean people like you have the right to harass him."

"People like me aren't bad compared to the police," Dave said. "I haven't told them the tie-in yet, Mrs. Ewing. From what your brother said, there didn't seem much reason to. He didn't act harassed. But you do. Why? No, let me tell you. You know something your brother doesn't. What is it, Mrs. Ewing? Were you on the extension phone Monday when Larry Johns asked Rick Wendell for fifteen hundred dollars?"

Dave heard her draw a sharp breath.

He said, "That's why you called me—right? To tell me about it?"

"Yes," she said. "No."

"I can send Lieutenant Yoshiba," he offered.

She said flatly, "Where are you? I don't want to talk here."

"It's lunchtime," he said. "There's a place called the Chardash, near the Los Santos Theater. They make a standout gypsy goulash."

"I'm not hungry," she said, "but I'll be there."

7

A campfire violin wept from a scratched record. Over a small, dark bar at the end of a shadowy room, a giant stein of German beer rippled in an electric sign. Dave sat on a stool with tubular metal legs that creaked and smoked a cigarette, drank gin and tonic, and talked to a stocky, middle-aged woman back of the bar. Sauces smeared her apron. Her round cheeks were flushed from stove heat. No other customers were in the place yet. She'd come out of the kitchen when the spring bell above the street door had jingled with his arrival.

"Monday night," he said. "She's a big old woman." He held out hands to measure Heather Wendell's bulk. "Big as a man. White hair. She cuts it short. It would have been around eight-thirty."

Round black eyes watched him, waiting.

"She'd have been with a small, dark man. Younger than she is. About forty. Black hair, combed forward." He stroked his own forehead. "Broken nose. Muscular." He made fists and revolved them in front of his chin. "A prize fighter, you understand? A boxer?"

"I understand," she said. "Yes, they here. I remember, because they order food and then do not eat. It make my husband angry." She smiled irony.

76

"Not with them. Never with customer, no. But with us. Me. Son. Daughter-in-law. When people will not eat, he become always angry, my husband."

"They talked," Dave said.

"Only talk." She nodded and started for the kitchen swing door. "You will excuse? I am alone."

"Did they leave together?" Dave called.

"I am sorry?" There was a clatter of metal, a hiss of steam. There were gusts of good smells. She reappeared with a deep, heavy saucepan in her hands, a big steel spoon. "What—I am sorry—you ask?"

"Did they go out together?"

"At the same time," she said. "They do not wait even for check. My daughter-in-law had not time to add up. And no one was at cash register." She nodded at it, glinting in the shadows near the door. "They leave ten-dollar bill and they go out." She twitched a harried smile and turned away again. "Excuse?"

Dave nodded. "Thank you." He stubbed out his cigarette, drank from the tinkling mint-sprigged glass, and the bell over the door jangled again. Sea light streamed in from the street. A bony blond woman in tailored green linen stood in it. The door fell shut and she came to him through the gloom. Her eyes were like her brother's—almost yellow. Only hers had no warmth in them. Neither had her voice. She said, "You're mistaken that I wanted to keep things from you."

"Mrs. Ewing?" Dave got off the stool. "What will you drink?"

"I won't," she said, "thank you. The reason I called you, Mr. Brandstetter, was to tell you about Larry

Johns. That what happened to him was his own doing and had nothing to do with Tom. Nothing."

"You mean the murder?"

She shook her head impatiently. "I don't know anything about that."

With a shrug, Dave tilted his head toward worn leather booths where unlit candles waited on checkered tablecloths. She hesitated, then went stiffly toward one in a corner. Taking his glass, he followed her, slid into the booth opposite her. "What is it you do know about?"

She laid a green handbag on the leather bench beside her, drew off green gloves and folded them on the bag. "I know he had visitors. Larry did."

Dave cocked an eyebrow. "At the beach house?"

"That morning. Monday. A man came, a big middle-aged man. In a dreadful purple satin shirt with embroidery. Cowboy outfit of some kind, I suppose. One of those LBJ hats. And the boots—tooled, you know? He needed a shave, his eyes were red. I didn't like the look of him. I don't approve of shouting in the house but I wouldn't have left him alone for a moment. Larry was with Tom." The corners of her mouth tightened bitterly. "I called his name and waited right there until he appeared. The man grinned all over his ugly face and spoke Larry's name and held out his hand but it was plain to me Larry had never seen him before. He approached with unmistakable caution."

Dave offered her a menu in a limp, fake leather folder. "What did he say?"

She shook her head at the menu. "I didn't wait

to hear. I went to see if Tom needed anything. Oh."
She lifted and let fall a hand. "I did hear a name.
Joe May. No . . ." She frowned to herself. "A single
word, I think. Jomay? Yes."

Dave took out his glasses, opened the folder, read
the food-spotted mimeographed sheet inside it.
"And what happened after that?"

Gail Ewing said, "They went out and walked on
the dunes. Right away. Larry obviously wanted the
man in the house no more than I did. I watched
them. Tom hadn't needed anything. I went upstairs.
They argued. It was plain from their gestures. The
man kept shaking a finger in Larry's face. At one
point they began shouting."

Dave pulled the glasses down his nose, looked at
her over the top of the menu. "Shouting what?"

"I can't say. It upset the dogs and they were barking.
It's impossible to hear anything once they begin." She
drew breath. "Anyway, soon Larry followed the man
out to the highway. Not, I'd say, willingly."

Dave set the menu back between the lightless
candle chimney and glass salt and pepper shakers.
"Out to the highway?"

"There was a camper parked there. Quite grimy.
When they got near it, a girl stepped down out of
the cab—a young woman. Larry stopped in his
tracks. From that moment on, the only one who
seemed to be talking was the man. He gesticulated
a good deal. Then the girl went to the back of the
camper and opened the door. At which point, Larry
turned and started to walk off."

Dave tilted up the last of his drink. "Go on."

"Well, the man lunged after him and caught his arm. Larry jerked free and came running for the house. Out the plank driveway Tom had built over the dunes. The man took half a dozen steps, then stopped and just stood there with Larry's jacket sleeve in his hand. The girl climbed out of the camper. Backward. I'm sure there was someone inside, someone she was coaxing to come out. But then the man went and spoke to her and she got back into the camper and shut the door and in a minute he drove the thing away."

The stout woman loomed out of the brown dimness now, holding an order pad and pencil. She'd left the soiled apron someplace. Dave said to Gail Ewing, "Sure you won't eat?" and at her headshake ordered for himself. The stout woman picked up Dave's empty glass and went away. Dave said, "And that was when Larry Johns called Rick Wendell—right?"

"I don't know whom he called," she said sharply. "I heard him come into the house by the door from the carport. And when I got downstairs, he was using the kitchen phone. I suppose he'd heard me on the stairs. He lowered his voice. But it was obvious that he was upset and the call was urgent."

"You didn't hear him mention money?"

"I heard him say his own name," she answered. "That's all. He repeated it several times. As if giving it to someone who'd never heard it before. I didn't lurk. The dogs and the children had given the living-room hard use on Sunday. I went to pick up. When Larry came out of the kitchen and saw me, he begged me not to tell Tom about the man who'd come to see him."

"And you didn't," Dave said. "Why?"

The yellow eyes went hard, the voice went hard. "Because he was in trouble and that was where I wanted him. Tom would only have rescued him. And I didn't want him rescued. I wanted him out."

"Which is also why you took the phone away from Tom when he saw the TV news and wanted to call a lawyer. And why you hung up on me when I phoned."

"People take advantage of Tom."

Dave's smile was thin. "Other people. Not you."

Her eyes widened, then narrowed. She said through clamped teeth, "What do you mean?"

"Why are we talking here? Why not at Tom Owens's house? At Tom Owens's bedside? Because you don't want him to know what you did to him. Not to Larry Johns—to him, your beloved brother."

She snatched up the gloves and purse. "I've never hurt Tom Owens in my life!" She slid out of the booth and stood, trembling. "Where do you think he'd be today if it weren't for me? You don't know him." Tears leaked down her face. Impatiently she knuckled them away. "He has no common sense, no sense of self-preservation. Without me to protect him—"

"Yes," Dave said. "He mentioned that. You've made a lot of decisions for him. That was a kind way of putting it. He strikes me as a kind man—taking you and Trudy in, supporting you all these years."

"He's very generous," she snapped.

"I'm not talking about nickels and dimes," Dave

81

said. "I'm talking about sacrificing any life of his own. He told me he'd never brought anybody home before Larry Johns."

"He has too much respect for me, for his family." She tugged the gloves on, motions jerky. Her voice sulked. "He could have done as he pleased. I never interfered. He'd no right to accuse me of that."

"Did you give him any encouragement?"

"Suppose I had." She was scornful. "You've seen an example of his taste and judgment. You've seen what Larry Johns turned out to be."

"I don't think he's a killer," Dave said.

"The police don't agree with you. Nor do I."

"The police are busy. And you don't like the boy. Those don't impress me as sufficient reasons to lock him up for the rest of his life."

She dug keys out of her bag and looked at him. "And your reason for defending him? Isn't it the same as Tom's? You're another of *those*, aren't you?"

"I try not to let it get in the way of my work," Dave said. "Mrs. Ewing, Larry Johns was simply a catalyst. His phone call from your kitchen triggered a chain reaction that ended in a man's death." Dave pushed out of the booth and stood facing her. "If you'd told your brother what you've told me here today, it's possible that man might still be alive."

Her mouth worked but she didn't answer. She turned and marched out into the street glare. Dave used a scarred black pay phone screwed to the wall by the cash register. Yoshiba was still out. He went back to the booth and ate his goulash.

82

8

Yoshiba said, "I checked you out." His hands were blocky like the rest of him. One of them shoved a bulging manila folder away from him on a crowded desktop. "With Ken Barker of the L.A.P.D. He votes for you. You're smart and you always win." He raked together a sprawl of ugly eight-by-tens—a half-naked female body dumped among ashcans—tamped their edges straight, set a telephone on them. He lifted a flat-nosed, expressionless face. "But to me you're a pain in the ass."

Dave shrugged. "You were the one who phoned me."

"Old lady Wendell wants me to post officers to keep you away from her place. Ace Kegan's lawyer wants me to get you off his back."

"Let me tell you about that pair."

When Dave had learned at the front desk that Yoshiba was back from lunch, he'd dropped coins into a glossy red machine in a tiled foyer under a Spanish dome and collected tall Cokes in flower-printed wax-paper cups. He set one of these in front of the Los Santos police lieutenant now, sat down, and told about Heather Wendell and Ace Kegan.

Yoshiba drank the Coke noisily and crunched the

ice chips. He dragged down the knot of his tie and unbuttoned the collar constricting his thick neck. He turned shirt sleeves up bulging forearms. He swiveled his chair to frown at the window. It was already open. Sun glared off ranks of parked cars outside.

"All right, all right," he said.

"When they got to the house in the canyon, things went wrong. They didn't want him dead. They only wanted to shock him out of wrecking everything they had together. A confrontation. It ended in a fight and sudden death. Which was why Kegan went home and drank himself senseless—a man who doesn't drink."

Yoshiba's blunt thumbnail peeled curls of wax off his cup. "And that call from Owens's kitchen—it was to the bar? And he gave Kegan his name?"

"And Kegan's lying. He knew that name. He told me himself Wendell was a loose talker. He'd told Kegan about Johns. Certainly Wendell and Johns weren't strangers meeting for the first time that night."

"So Kegan smelled trouble, the same old kind, right? And checked the bank on a hunch and learned about the fifteen hundred. Why didn't he tell Mrs. Wendell?"

"Maybe he didn't have to," Dave said. "Maybe she knew it first and told him."

Yoshiba shook his head. "No good. She'd have mentioned robbery to me."

"Why? Johns obviously didn't have the money. It would have messed up a simple case and put her and Kegan in the middle. She was careless, leaving that empty envelope there. But no more careless than you were."

Something glinted in Yoshiba's black eyes. "I

84

wasn't trying to save my company twenty-five big bills." He shook his head. "It's frail, Brandstetter. I mean, it's abnormal psychology, for Christ sake. I've got a suspect locked in. What do I need with abnormal psychology? I'm working sixteen hours a day now." He lifted and dropped the heavy manila folder. "This is new today. This whole stack. The gun was in the kid's hand."

"But your own lab says he didn't fire it."

"Hoo." Yoshiba blew out air and stood up. "You've only got the Ewing woman's word for the phone call. And she didn't hear anything about money. That could have been exactly like Kegan told it—to buy hot furniture off a truck."

"To revamp an already revamped bar?" Dave said. "Let's ask the boy."

"Impossible," Yoshiba said. "The D.A.—"

Dave stood up. "Owens didn't get him a lawyer, so what he's got is the public defender, right? Down the hall? What's the P.D.'s name? He'll go for this, if you won't."

"Khazoyan is his name." Yoshiba leaned out the window and drew deep breaths. He pulled his head in. "Sure, he'll go for it. A lawyer with a client who won't even talk to him? He'll kiss you on both cheeks. But you have to jump over the D.A. first."

"Not if you don't tell him," Dave said.

"You want a lot for a Coke," Yoshiba said. But he grinned.

Khazoyan's hair was silken and thinning. He was olive-skinned, had a thick, high-bridged nose and sunken cheeks. He slouched in a fake-leather swivel chair like Yoshiba's, with his feet on a desk stacked higher with paper than Yoshiba's. He wore new blunt-toed shoes with one-inch soles and two-inch heels. His shirt was lace. He ate a corned-beef sandwich on rye bread that was disintegrating. He licked mayonnaise and mustard from thin fingers and stretched a tired arm for a paper cup of coffee on his desk. His eyes were brown, bulging and luminous. His voice was tired as his motions, weak, high and hoarse. Above a very wide knotted necktie his larynx jumped as if it were trying to escape.

"Yeah, it sounds important. He won't tell you, though. He won't tell anybody anything. He must have been jolted out of his mind—always supposing he's got a mind—when that old woman walked in on him. Otherwise he'd never have told her his name. He sure as hell never told anyone else. She told Yoshiba. For all the kid said, she could have made it up. If it weren't for his driver's license, I wouldn't believe it."

"He also has a local habitation," Dave said, "and a history. Those people in the camper are part of it. Which also makes them part of his future."

"Metaphysics." Khazoyan worked black brows, pushed the last bite of sandwich into his mouth, got his feet down off the desk. He sat forward and, while he chewed, wiped his hands on a meager paper napkin. He drained off the rest of his coffee, dropped the balled napkin into the cup, let the cup fall under the desk, where a metal wastebasket clanked. He got to his feet. "Okay." A jacket with tiny flowers stitched into the weave lay over the back of a metal chair. He pulled it on. "Let's give it a try." He opened the door into the hall.

Larry Johns said, "The sarape and the hat. They're Tom's. Will you take them back to him?"

When Dave had described the boy to Ace Kegan, he'd only seen a police photograph, read a police description. Johns was slighter than Bobby Reich. He looked frail, seated in faded Levi's and wilted T-shirt and scuffed cowboy boots on a stiff chair in a bare white room. He faced Dave and Khazoyan across an empty table. His long, straw-color hair was snarled. There was patchy beard stubble at the point of his chin. His eyes looked bruised.

Dave told him, "Maybe you can take them back to him yourself soon. Why did you wear them?"

"That son of a bitch Huncie tore the sleeve off my windbreaker," Johns said. "Tom bought me a suit but you don't hustle johns in a suit. And it's cold at the beach at night. I had to wear something. Besides—" But he moved a hand instead of finishing the sentence.

"Yes?" Dave said. "The hat?"

The boy sat forward, looked at the square red tiles of the floor, moved his thin shoulders, mumbled, "I wanted to wear something of his. I wasn't leaving. I just had to get some bread fast, that was all." He looked up. "I'd never leave Tom. Tom's the best thing that ever happened to me." The blue eyes were miserably earnest. "He liked that sarape and that hat. I don't know—it made me feel like I wasn't really going anyplace."

87

"But you were," Dave said. "Who saw you?"

"Nobody. Tom was asleep. Doped. He took pills when the itching got too bad—you know, his legs, those casts. There's stairs up to the deck, around the corner from his room. I left that way."

"And waited on the coast road for Wendell?"

"He was there. He said eight and I was a minute late."

"I'd like an explanation," Dave said.

The blue eyes turned reproachful. They looked guardedly at Khazoyan, who was using a yellow pencil on a long yellow pad, then back at Dave. "He said he'd give me the money I needed."

"Fifteen hundred dollars," Dave said. "For what? And why Wendell? Why not Owens? He was your friend."

The boy's face closed. "I couldn't ask him for money. Not Tom. What we had wasn't like that."

"So he told me," Dave said. "But that's not all of it, is it? You didn't want him to know what the money was for. You were afraid to tell him."

Khazoyan stopped writing and lifted his head.

The boy looked at him, at Dave. Unhappier than he'd looked till now. He got out of the chair and stood at the window, back to them. He said, "Yeah. Okay. You're right. Well, Jesus." He turned back, hands held out. "It was for child-support payments. To my ex-wife."

Dave half smiled. "What had you told Owens you were—a virgin?"

"No, but—Tom's got high standards. I'd run out on my responsibilities—right? Anyway, I'm living off him. What am I supposed to do—lay a wife and baby on him too?"

"The girl in the camper," Dave said.

"Jomay," Johns said sourly. "And BB. She dragged BB all the way here. To show me how big she is now. That was when I took off. If I wanted to know how big she was, for Christ sake, I knew where to find her. That creep Huncie. Jomay'd never have found me by herself."

"Huncie?" Khazoyan wondered.

"'Uncle' Dwayne Huncie," Johns said disgustedly. "The turnip-nosed old son of a bitch. He's running a game. Calls himself a lawyer. Specializes in tracking down husbands that skip. But I'll bet he takes most of what he collects. Fees, you know? Plus which I bet he lays her every chance he gets, in that camper."

"Only this time he didn't collect," Khazoyan said.

"He would have. He leaned hard. And what could I do? I owed it. Jomay's old lady owns three beauty parlors. She didn't need it. But the judge said I had to pay it. So I thought of Rick and I promised Huncie I'd have the bread for him next morning. He'd have braced Tom for it otherwise. I told him there was some other dude who said he'd give me money anytime I asked. I'd get it from him."

"Did you give him Wendell's name?" Dave asked.

"I had to," Johns said. "Huncie's a mean bastard. He wasn't buying anything vague. Didn't trust me. He wanted to know exactly who and how and when."

"Did you give him Wendell's address?"

"I didn't know it then—only the bar. I gave him the name of the bar—The Hang Ten."

"The home address is in the phone book," Khazoyan said wearily. "So you told this Huncie character where you were going to get his fifteen hundred dollars."

"How did you know Wendell would come through?" Dave asked. "That's a lot of money."

Johns eyed him bleakly. "It's what he told me. The one time we made it. He took me home from The Hang Ten. Afterward he said if I'd keep doing it with him, he'd give me anything I wanted. I said I wasn't ready. Anytime, he said. All I had to do was ask. So—" He watched Khazoyan take out cigarettes, light one, put the pack away, start writing again, squinting an eye against the smoke from the cigarette in the corner of his mouth. Dave held out his pack to Johns. The boy took a cigarette, tried for a smile and missed.

"So?" Dave snapped the lighter for him.

Johns said dully, "So I asked." He lit the cigarette, took it from his mouth and looked at it. "Thanks."

"You telephoned the bar first," Dave said.

The door opened behind him. Johns looked over Dave's head but he answered, "He wasn't there yet. Gail keeps all the clocks set fast. Ten minutes. I kept forgetting. So I phoned his house. Rick's."

"Who answered?" Yoshiba asked from the doorway. Down the hall back of him a child was crying.

"His mother," Johns said.

Dave and Khazoyan spoke together and stopped.

The door clicked shut and Yoshiba stood at Dave's elbow. "Did you give her your name?"

"Sure," Johns said. "She asked. Why not?"

"You never gave us your name." Yoshiba swung a thick thigh onto a corner of the table. "You opened up to her. Did you tell her what you wanted with her son?"

"Watch that," Khazoyan said to his tablet.

"Forget it," Yoshiba said.

"I didn't tell her anything," Johns said. "I told Rick when he got on the phone. He was cheered up. Wow! I felt like a shit. Because I wasn't going to stay with him. I was going to do it that night and take the bread and he wasn't ever going to see me again."

"That worked out," Yoshiba said.

Johns gave him a disgusted look. He said to Dave, "But I was in a bind. What could I do? I don't mean I wasn't going to pay him back. I'd have paid him back."

"All right," Yoshiba cut in. "He gave you the money. What did you do with it? Shove it up your ass?"

"Watch that," Khazoyan droned again.

"He showed it to me when we got there," Johns said hotly. "He opened the envelope and showed it to me. In twenties, all neat, with those paper bands around the bundles, you know? That was what Huncie asked for—cash, small bills. So Rick got it that way. New twenty-dollar bills. You can tell Huncie is crooked. Who asks for money in cash, you know? That much money? Why not a check made out to Jomay? I mean, it's her bread, right? By the law—every second word Huncie says is 'law'—it's Jomay's money. And BB's."

"Beebee?" Yoshiba looked and sounded blank.

"The baby. She's eighteen months old."

Yoshiba said, "He wanted you to make child payments—this Huncie?"

Khazoyan in his hoarse high voice gave the lieutenant the facts. Yoshiba said, "Good grief."

Dave said gently, "He showed you the money? Took it out of the envelope, then put it back? What?"

"Well"—Johns squirmed on the chair, his tired young face flushing—"he had his mind on"—thin fingers tugged at the straggly mustache—"on what he brought me there for. I mean, the money wasn't going anyplace."

"It went," Khazoyan said. "You didn't notice it was missing when you came out of the bedroom?"

"With him laying there on the floor with blood pouring out of his chest?" Johns frowned. "Was it missing?"

"It still is," Khazoyan said.

Dave said, "Huncie told you to deliver the money Tuesday morning. To him. Where?"

"He was coming back for it. To Tom's, the beach house. Ten o'clock."

Dave pushed his chair back. The worn rubber leg tips stuttered on the tiles. He stood up, touched Yoshiba's bulky shoulder. "May I use your phone?"

"Help yourself," Yoshiba said. And to Johns, "How come you open up today? I'm a nice fellow. What is it—you don't trust Orientals? Why cover up all this time and break out for him?"

"I was trying to protect Tom," Johns said.

"Now that doesn't mean anything. He found out about Tom."

Tom Owens answered the phone. The barking of the dogs echoed off the hard inlets and tall groins of the wooden house. "Gail isn't here," he said, "but I've been trying to reach you. Shall we say frantically? There's a girl here, young woman. Claims she's Larry's wife, ex-wife. She's got a baby with her. Says it's Larry's. She says he was going to get money for her—money he owed her. Court-ordered. Fifteen hundred dollars."

"I've been talking to him," Dave said. "I know."

"There was some man," Owens said, "helping her."

"Dwayne Huncie," Dave said. "Is he there?"

"No. Wait a minute. I'll put the girl on."

When Dave walked back into the interrogation room, Yoshiba was sitting on the floor, clasping thick knees in thick arms, his back against the wall, and staring up from that bland moon face of his at Larry Johns, still on the chair. Dave told him:

"You might put out an all-points bulletin for a camper with Texas license plates, registered to Dwayne Huncie."

"He'll be back in Texas," Yoshiba protested. "It will take a month and letters from two governors to get him back here. What are you trying to say— that this Huncie walked in and picked up the money while Johns and Wendell were doing it in the next room?"

Dave looked at Johns. "Did you hear anything?"

"Before what I told the cops? Well, yeah. Yeah." He sat straight, excited. "I heard something. I said, 'What's that? Somebody's out there.' Rick just said for me to stop being so nervous and relax. So I did. But the next time, he heard it too. And we both knew somebody was out there. And he went out to see. And that was when I heard voices and the gun went off."

"How long after the first time?" Yoshiba asked.

"Aw, hell." The frail shoulders lifted and fell. He'd smoked the cigarette down short. He leaned to snub it out in the chipped ashtray on the table. "I wasn't exactly looking at my watch right then. Five minutes?"

Yoshiba stood up. "So Huncie came after the kid here to make sure of getting the money and Wendell came out and caught him and tried to stop him with the gun and Huncie turned it on him?"

"Huncie can tell you," Dave said. "Find Huncie."

"Even if we got extradition," Yoshiba said, "it would cost a bundle to get him here—jet fares for him and two guards. This is a small town, Brandstetter."

Dave shook his head. "Huncie has a brother in Saugus. He'd spoken of going there."

"Spoken? Who to? Who did you just telephone?"

"Tom Owens. Jomay Johns is at his house. Now."

Larry Johns groaned and held his head.

Dave said, "Monday night, Huncie picked her and the baby up at a theater where he'd parked them. About eleven. They went to a McDonald's. He'd been crying about being broke but that night he peeled a twenty-dollar bill off a big fat roll and gave it to her to pay for their hamburgers. Then he excused himself to go to the men's room. And never came back."

"I'll put out the APB." Yoshiba went to the door. "But only for California."

"It was an Indian Head camper," Larry Johns said. "On an old orange Chevy pickup with a smashed headlight."

Yoshiba opened the door. "License number?"

"You're kidding," the boy said. Yoshiba grunted and left. The boy looked at Dave with tear-filled eyes. "You're really something else," he said. "You're going to get me out of this."

"Don't count on it," Dave said. "Not yet."

Outside in the corridor, a knee-high child bumped into him. It wore a T-shirt with orange juice stains and little Levi's that looked ready to fall off. A fist held a grubby string. The string dragged a yellow wooden duck. On its side. Dave crouched and set it on its red wooden wheels. The child went off down the hall without any change of expression. The duck's head turned around as it traveled. The wheels made a clacking sound and a small bell jingled.

Dave was watching it and laughing to himself when a door opened near the end of the hall. Vern Taylor came out in his nice new sneakers. He didn't look Dave's way. He went ahead of the child toward open doors at the end of the corridor. He went out the doors down a walk between hibiscus bushes with flowers red as his windbreaker jacket. He went off up a sunlit street.

Dave thought he wanted to look at the door. PAROLE was lettered on its fogged glass. That was interesting. He hadn't expected anything interesting from Vern Taylor. He went inside. A woman with faded red hair worked an electric typewriter at a desk off the same assembly line as Yoshiba's and Khazoyan's, even to the piled-up papers. She bent her head and looked at him over wire-rimmed goggles she'd pulled down on a long, thin nose. Her eyebrows asked what he wanted.

He laid down a card. "The P.O. handling Vern Taylor?"

The offices were boxed off by partitions, wood below, frosted glass above. The one the woman nodded him to was big enough for what it held and no more—a file cabinet, a desk, two chairs. And a small man who looked no heavier than the weight of his bones, there was so little but bones to him. He pushed a manila folder into a file drawer, rolled the drawer shut, turned. And jerked his bald head in surprise.

"Dave Brandstetter! Long time."

He came around the desk, smiling, holding out a hand. Dave shook it carefully. It felt frangible. "Years," he said. "So this is where they stuck you."

The man's name was Squire. It had been a couple of decades since Dave had begun asking him questions. He made a wry face. "I asked for it. Thought it would be different from L.A. It's the same." He sat in the swivel chair behind the desk. "Probably be the same anyplace. Sit down. You like coffee or something?" He started to get up again.

Dave shook his head and dropped onto the other chair. "What I'd like is what I always like from you. Information that's none of my business. I just saw Vern Taylor walk out of here. Why?"

"He'll be walking in and out of here every week for the next two years. I'm not sure it'll be enough. On the record, he needs a keeper." Squire took the folder out of the cabinet again and sat down again. "He just came out of Chino." Squire opened the folder, put on dime-store reading glasses, the kind with lenses like dry half moons, leaned forward, blinking while he leafed over the papers the folder held. "Ah, it's pathetic. Felonies, yeah, but 288.A, for Christ sake." The number was from the California Penal Code. It stood for oral copulation. "Plus 290." That meant failure to register as a sex offender. "Because his record goes back. A long time." He took the glasses off. "You want it all?"

"I don't know why," Dave said. "But yes, if you're not too busy. I'm into a case that's like a jigsaw too many little kids have fooled with on too many rainy Sunday afternoons. Half the pieces are missing. Taylor probably isn't one of them. I can't see where he'd fit but he is underfoot. Let's hear it."

Squire put the glasses back on, peered at the papers again, drew a deep breath and let it out windily. "Okay. He's been in sex scrapes starting twelve, fifteen years ago. Parks, bus station men's rooms, the old familiar places. The Astor Bar on

Main Street. Always 647.A." It was the code for solicitation to commit a lewd act. "Misdemeanors, right? You pay a little fine and walk out after a night in the slams. But if your employer learns about it you can lose out. He had a good job. Civil service. Second bust, they found out and shed him."

"Drafting," Dave said.

Squire's mild eyes peered at him over the glasses. "You know all this?"

"Almost none of it," Dave said. "Go on."

"By not mentioning his arrest record and because nobody checked, he got on with a private building contractor. Three more arrests. Somehow he kept it from them. But on number four some bastard in the Department made sure they heard all about it."

"Friendly," Dave said.

"Well, Christ," Squire said. "Taylor had to know it was a losing game. Didn't he? Dave, what the hell is the matter with those people?"

"They're crazy," Dave said. "Like the rest of us."

"Not like the rest of us," Squire said, "or there wouldn't be laws against it." He sighed and picked up the papers again. "Then, believe it or not, he tried teaching. No shit. Summer term, high school. I doubt they'd ever have found out except a bar was raided. The Black Cat, on Sunset. You remember that?"

"How many arrests did they make that night? Twenty?"

"And all the names got in the papers," Squire said. "Which put an end to his teaching career. And respectability, if that's the word. The next arrest was a 647.B."

"Prostitution?" Dave said.

"I guess he still looked young," Squire said. "Anyway, he was living off it. If you call a room at the Ricketts Hotel living." The place was six sagging stories of dingy brick standing to its knees in a wash of greasy neon on Los Angeles's skid row. "He'd score in the Astor downstairs and take the johns up to the room. Only one night he chose the wrong trick. A vice squad officer."

"A felony," Dave said. "What did he draw?"

"That woman lawyer, the one with the two Persian cats she always took into court on silver chains," Squire said. "She bargained him out. But it cost him."

"The Duchess," Dave said. "Those Pershing Square faggots worshiped her and she exploited them down to their last rhinestone. We should all have friends like May Sweeny."

"So he tried for a real job again. Through one of those gay social service agencies. They put him in a candy factory run by two old aunties who didn't give a damn about his record. But they only paid a buck an hour."

"I know the place," Dave said. "And how privileged the boys feel. So how did he end in Chino? When?"

"A year ago last December," Squire said. "Christmas Eve, God help us. They busted him on 288.A. In an alley doorway back of a garment place on Broadway. In the rain. Oral copulation in the rain, no less. He came up before Judge Macander and you know what happened. Macander read his record"—Squire rattled the typed sheet at Dave—"and gave him five years and a thousand dollars."

"And he just got out?" Dave asked.

"About a month ago," Squire said. "Back to the Ricketts but not for long. He changed bases and he's in Surf, so I inherited him."

"Macander wanted jail to straighten him out," Dave said. "Forty years of disappointments haven't dimmed his faith in jails. Did it work?"

Squire shut the folder and got up to put it away again and to shut the file drawer. "He thinks it was bad luck. All his life it's been bad luck. Not bad judgment, not stupidity, not failure to learn from life. Just bad luck."

"Yup." Dave rose. "If he'd been born rich, none of it would have happened, right?"

Squire dropped the dime-store glasses on the desk. "You've talked to him. You didn't need all this."

"I guess not," Dave said. "I don't know what to do with it." He went to the office door. "Come on, let me buy you a drink."

"Like old times," Squire said, and came with him.

9

A square package stood on his desk. Brown paper. Twine. It was alone there. He kept the desktop empty. It was a good-looking desk that he'd hunted a long time to find. Slabs of oiled teak hung in a brushed steel frame. Door whispering shut behind him, he frowned and went grimly down the long, cold room. He kept the thermostat low. Somebody had asked him once, "What do you do—hang beef in here?" Doug, he supposed. Doug had accused him before and since of subnormal warmth.

He put on his horn rims and picked up the package. The label was neatly lettered but without a return address. He held it to his ear. Nothing ticked inside. But maybe this one wasn't meant to tick. Maybe opening it was what would trigger it. He dropped into a saddle leather chair that turned its back to a glass wall that showed blank blue sky, a lone helicopter. Out of a deep drawer he lifted his phone but he didn't dial. His father came in.

Carl Brandstetter was a straight, ruddy man of sixty-five with handsome white hair, blue eyes and an expensive tailor. He turned back to say something out the door, let it fall shut, nodded to Dave and walked to a cabinet where liquor, ice, glasses hid themselves behind insulated steel finished to look like wood. He bent to open doors and take out bottles. "Go on with your call."

"It can wait." Dave stood. "What did the doctor tell you?"

"To stop smoking." Carl Brandstetter snorted, dropped miniature ice cubes into a pitcher of thick Danish crystal. "And drinking." He measured gin with a squat glass jigger. "And working." He measured vermouth, set the bottles back, found a jar of stuffed olives, shut the door. "And sex." From the snowy little cave that was the freezer compartment he took stem glasses and dropped an olive into each.

Dave said, "That doesn't leave you many options."

"Backgammon." His father moved the crowded ice with a glass rod. "At the senior citizen center. And a little light shuffleboard, maybe once a week." He poured from the pitcher, turned, smiling, holding out a frost-crusted glass to Dave. "But no tournaments. Nothing to work up the adrenaline."

"Heart?" Dave took the glass, tasted the drink.

"It appears to be broken." Carl Brandstetter sat in a white goat-hide chair and placed his glass on a low glass-and-steel table where an Aztec metate— rough gray stone on three legs—was the ashtray. "That would give some women in this city a laugh."

"It was always *their* hearts," Dave said. There had been nine of them, if you included only wives. Carl Brandstetter wasn't a collector—he was a discarder. Dave watched him start a cigarette with a gold lighter that for shape and incising matched his cuff links. "You're smoking. You're drinking."

The older man said, "I feel fine. When I'm dead I'll no doubt think giving it up would have been worth it. Right now, it's unreal. The sun is shining. I have a lovely and devoted young wife who will stop in the Bentley shortly to drive me to dinner at—"

"The women," Dave said, "it won't matter a damn to. It will matter to me."

The board chairman of Medallion Life raised white brows. "Sentimentality? From you?"

"Just fact," Dave said. "Why not cut down a little?"

"What's in the package?" his father wondered.

Dave sipped his drink. "Do we own a metal detector?"

"Not that I know of. Why?" Carl Brandstetter rose, hefted the parcel, read the label. "Hmm. Anonymous."

"It's possible somebody would like me dead," Dave told him. "It's happened before—remember?"

"On this Wendell matter?" Carl Brandstetter set down the box, went to pick up his glass. "I'm told there's been static. The mother is turning attorneys loose on us. The business partner wants you fired."

"I'm still not sure those two didn't kill him." Dave lit a cigarette, sat on a desk corner, spelled out his reasons. "But there are new characters in the drama. A little ex-wife from Texas. The suspect's. Her baby and her backwoods lawyer, demanding fifteen hundred dollars in delinquent child-support payments."

He went on with that part of the story while Carl

Brandstetter took a gold penknife from a pocket and cut the twine on the package. He folded back the brown paper. More twine bound the carton inside. He cut this too, folded the knife blade with a click, put the knife away. He grinned at Dave. "You don't want to leave the room?"

Dave said, "You never did have any imagination."

"You've got enough for both of us," his father said. "The Johns boy killed him. It's more obvious now than before. The fifteen hundred dollars was the motive."

"He didn't get it," Dave said. "Who did?"

"I'd suggest you ask the first police officer on the scene. They're badly paid." Carl Brandstetter opened the flaps of the carton and pulled out fistfuls of shredded paper. Dave leaned to look inside. What rested there was a handsome pot in brown and black glazes. A three-inch envelope gleamed in the bottom of the pot. He thumbed it open, slid out a linen-finish card.

With half my love—Kovaks.

His father was watching him quizzically. Dave handed him the card. "Half?" Carl Brandstetter asked.

"The other half is for Doug," Dave said.

His father grimaced and handed back the card. "You should get out of that life." He went back to the goat-hair chair, walking heavily, sitting heavily. Magazines lay on the table, three issues of *Apollo*, large and thick and glossy. He leafed one over. Dave glimpsed Queen Anne legs, broken-faced Greek marbles, plummy 1890s English genre paintings.

Carl Brandstetter said without looking up, "You plan to go free lance when I die, I hope. Because you know the board will fire you. And why."

Dave shrugged. "I like the job," he said. "But I feel about it the way you feel about your heart. I'm not ready to give up my sex life for it."

When he opened the palsied aluminum screen door of Sawyer's Pet Shop, small birds flew up like scraps of colored paper in the window. The window was backed by wire mesh. The space made a flight cage for parakeets and finches. There were crooked stick perches, little wooden ladders, hanging gourds, hollowed out and gaily painted. The sheet-metal floor was graveled, strewn with grain and dried corn. Button quail pecked there.

Along one wall of the shop bubbled aquariums filled with wavery green light and the dim dream dartings of improbable fish. Along the other wall shelves held cans of dog food, boxes of birdseed, cuttlebone, catnip, spray-can deodorants and mange cures. Wire racks on swivels were hung with plastic-bagged sticks and knots of hide for dogs to chew, rubber bones, flannel mice, collars rhinestoned, studded, belled, bright leashes of dyed leather, glittering chain leashes. Shiny new cages hung from the ceiling. Cat pans in gaudy molded plastic were stacked on the floor between dog baskets and heaps of heavy printed paper sacks of cat sand and kibble.

Canaries sang. The little parrots and finches kept up a shrill clamor. Kittens mewed. Pups whined. Gerbils ran in squeaky wheels. Tiny spotted mice pirouetted in the sawdust of glass boxes. Cavies hopped over the backs of stony gopher tortoises munching trampled lettuce. Doug Sawyer punched a cash register, blinked at Dave, and went on talking with a woman in pants and hair curlers who held by its leather handle a cat carrier of new plywood and bright screen.

Doug's little mother, in her flowered smock, peered with her one bright bird eye from the back room. A brown-and-white young rabbit was cradled in her arm. Her free hand held a medicine dropper. She gave Dave a smile of bright false teeth and lifted her chin, summoning him. The back room smelled of wood shavings and alfalfa. Tarnished cages went up the walls—parrots, monkeys, a hunched and scraggly raven, a cross-eyed Siamese cat who paced.

"I hope you can forgive me," Belle Sawyer said. She kept a hot plate on a shelf and a glass pot of water always simmered for coffee. Bottles of instant mix and powdered cream substitute and a box of cube sugar grew dusty there. A small pan with some glutinous carroty substance covered the second burner now. Into this the pet shop woman dipped the medicine dropper, filled it, edged its tip in at a corner of the young rabbit's mouth. The brown nose twitched. The plush little body struggled. "I'm always keeping Doug." The thick glasses glittered up at Dave. One lens had white cloth neatly pasted inside it. She'd lost an eye to a hawk's talon years ago. "He can't get on with his own life at all. I hope you know I don't mean it." She rubbed the rabbit's fur throat, smiled satisfaction when it swallowed, and murmured comfort to it.

"Maybe it's over for a while now. It's my circulation. Old age. Too many years on my feet here, I suppose. Whatever, the veins don't let the blood through to my brain." She filled the dropper again and gently squeezed the liquid into the rabbit's mouth. It shook its ears. They made sounds like big moth wings. "There, that's enough for now." She bent, dropped it into a cage, where it crouched in shavings and shredded paper. She clicked the wire door shut. There was a stained and meager sink with a steel tap. The plumbing shuddered when she turned it on to rinse the medicine dropper.

"Coffee?" She didn't wait for his answer. She used a cracked plastic spoon to dip brown powder into a plastic mug. Pouring in water, she said, "It's so maddening, because it all seems quite serious and normal when I'm going through it. I was President this week—I expect Doug told you. And I really did issue orders, stacks of them, that everything was to be 'all right.' Can you imagine?" She clicked the spoon busily in the mug and handed it to Dave. Her bright eye mocked. "I felt so confident, so secure. I haven't felt that way since Mr. Sawyer was alive." Her mouth turned down in a wry smile. "But of course it was all a delusion. Even the Capitol at Mount Rushmore. You know, where the Presidents are carved in the mountain?"

"The Black Hills." Dave blew at his sudsy coffee.

"That's it." She nodded. "I'd moved the government to the Black Hills. For safety. The coasts are sinking into the sea." She laughed. "Aren't they?"

"Hold the thought." Dave lit a cigarette. "But it goes away?"

"Exactly like a dream," she said. "I'm nervous, of course. I must have mailed those presidential orders. I don't have the least idea to whom. I hope I simply made up names and addresses but it seems to me one went to the Queen of England. Dr. Simpson says I probably didn't stamp them—a President doesn't have to. Heavens! The Black Hills. I've never even been there!"

Doug stood in the doorway. "She's okay," he said.

"Looks that way," Dave said. "That's good."

"I'll be all right now." But her chirpiness didn't last. "Oh, dear. I've said that before, haven't I?"

Doug said, "Don't worry about it. That's the main thing. It's not your fault. And it's not hurting anybody, right?" He put an arm around her shoulders, kissed her frizzy dandelion hair. "Whoo! Glover's dog soap!" He wrinkled his nose, rubbed it with the back of a hand.

"You know that's what I've always used. Made you use it too, when you were little enough for me to boss you."

"They barked at me in third grade," Doug said.

"Nonsense," she said. "It's a good, clean smell. And it's very healthy for the hair."

Doug looked at his watch and at Dave. "Four forty-five. You want to finish that?"

"There's no need," Belle Sawyer said. "I know it's terrible stuff." She reached for the mug and

Dave let her take it because she was right, it was terrible.

Doug crouched by the rabbit cage. "How's he doing?"

"Who can say? They're so delicate." She touched his shoulder. "You run along. I'll close up. I feel absolutely sane." She smiled at Dave. "It's not as much fun as being President." She frowned to herself. "I don't think I even had a Congress. Just me, in the oval office, signing orders. And everything was going to be just fine."

They left her standing in the shop doorway, a small hand lifted, and smiling wistfully at nothing.

The stereo components sat on the bare floor in the big, empty front room. From them echoed the heartbreak of the Haydn Symphony 93 *largo cantabile*. The old gent had been homesick in the London of 1791 and mocked his loneliness with that wry bassoon honk at the end. Dave smiled at it when he came out of the shower and shrugged into his terry-cloth robe. He lit a cigarette, picked up from the floor beside the bed this week's *New York Review* and headed for the kitchen. Before he got there, the whine of the blender motor cut through the music. Wincing, he walked into the good onion, garlic, fried chicken smells of the high, tiled room.

"You like *poule à la mexicaine?*" Doug, in a faded denim happy coat, mop of gray hair still wet from his shower, went to the refrigerator. "Then don't make faces. I have to purée the pimientos."

Dave eyed the little orange-pink storm in the jar

atop the infernal machine with its row of color-coded push buttons. "That's puréeing?"

"Among us twentieth-century types." Doug handed him a martini. "It'll be over in just a minute."

Dave grunted, took the martini and, with the paper tucked under his arm, wandered out to crank the painty old latch of the twin French doors to the roof deck. He shouldered them open and started for the redwood chaise, chair, table in the big leaf shadows of the rubber trees. He stopped. At the far end of the deck, something glared in the downing sunlight. Squinting, he went toward it. It was square, about four feet high, maybe a yard wide, forty inches deep—pale brick sheathed in shiny plate steel, a rectangular opening in the top, steel doors in the front, stumps of lead pipe at the side.

Around this were piled cartons full of big Mason jars, labeled with chemical names, holding colored powders. There was a gathering of plastic trash barrels in dull green dribbled with duller gray. Slip was what they'd held, liquid pottery clay. Under a shelter built of four-by-fours and roofed with rippled sheets of hard opalescent plastic, where plank shelves were meant for potted plants—a project he and Doug hadn't got to yet—terra-cotta-colored molds for pots and jars waited beside a clay-crusty potter's wheel with a little electric motor under it, trailing a cracked rubber coated cord.

Dave blinked, frowned, worked his teeth together gently. He drank the martini, slowly, smoked the cigarette down. He took it to the ashtray on the table to crush it out. Leaving the paper but taking his empty glass, he went back into the apartment, back into the kitchen. He said very mildly, "Doug?"

Doug, at the stove, wiped sweat from his face with his sleeve. "Something wrong?"

"What does a potter's kiln look like?"

"Kind of like an oven." Doug reached down a can of chicken broth from a cupboard shelf. The electric can opener sang and danced with it. "Brick, I think. Why?"

"There's one on the roof deck." Dave opened the fridge and refilled his glass. Doug's stood cradling a drying olive on the tile counter next to the stove. He floated the olive again and put the pitcher back. "At least I think so. Whatever it is, it must weigh a ton."

Doug emptied the gold-lumped broth into the skillet, where it sizzled gently. He poured in the pimiento purée. "On our roof deck?"

"Yonder." Dave pointed. "You didn't know?"

"How would I know? I've been away since eight-thirty this morning. I hope that old idiot in the bicycle shop is more alert than he looks. I told him to keep an eye on her and let me know." Doug spooned into the skillet yellow-green powder from a small jar. Cumin. He opened his eyes at Dave. "You think I put it there?"

"We both know who put it there," Dave said. "I just had a laughable idea that he might have asked permission. But of course that's ridiculous."

Doug carried the cumin jar and the spoon out of the kitchen, out the French doors, and down the deck. He stopped, shook his head, said something about *merde*.

"He didn't have permission?" Dave asked.

"Of course not." Doug touched the pale brick, the steel sheathing. "My God, how do you suppose he got it up here? Look at the thing."

"At least a ton," Dave said. "And he's moved his whole shop here with it—molds, wheel, clay, the works."

"It was default," Doug said suddenly. "He told me, Dave. I thought it was fact. It wasn't fact, it was a warning, only I was too dense to take it in. The place where he had his shop is being torn down. Some old warehouse in east Santa Monica. He had to get out."

"Fine," Dave said, "but he didn't ask—"

"If he'd asked, I'd have asked you," Doug said.

Dave eyed him. "But you'd have considered it."

"Maybe." Doug shrugged. "I don't know. It never crossed my mind." He smiled, touched Dave's face. "What do you think? I don't want Kovaks. I like his work is all. We've been over that."

"He intends to stay," Dave said.

"Well, I guess it wouldn't hurt, would it? I mean, if he wants to work here, there's plenty of space."

"You tell him he can work here, and next week he'll be living here. That's all it's about." Dave went back into the hollow rooms, into the shimmer of Haydn's strings, and fetched the pot in its carton from where he'd set it down at the stairhead. Doug was in the kitchen again. Dave showed him the carton, the pot, the card. "The lunatic wants to sleep between us."

"I guess so." Doug frowned while he used a long-handled wooden spoon to move the chunks of chicken around in the thick pale-red sauce with its snippets of green pepper. "I got one too. Yesterday. It came with the rest of the gallery packages. By United Parcel."

"Same card, right?" Dave asked.

"Same card." Kovaks showed his beautiful teeth in the kitchen doorway. "Am I in time for a drink? I'm pooped." He wore dirty white duck shorts. A dirty white yachting cap was stuck on the back of his bushy hair. Sweat greased his pale skin. He held out grimy hands. "Why aren't you cheering?"

"How long did it take to get that kiln up here?"

"Over four hours, a power winch, and three hairy hardhats. Tell you the truth, I didn't think we'd get done before you showed up. They weren't expensive enough. They kept stopping for beers."

"Let me guess," Dave said. "Paying them took your last dime, correct?"

"Absolutely correct. You're uncanny." Kovaks found the martini pitcher in the refrigerator and a frosty glass in the freezer compartment. He filled the glass. "I don't know where I'd have turned to if it wasn't for friends like you."

"Help yourself to a drink," Dave said. "Make yourself right at home. But you look tired and hot. Wouldn't you like a shower? Sure, you would."

Kovaks stood very still, watching him. Doug watched him too. He asked Doug cheerily:

"There's plenty of chicken, isn't there?" He didn't wait for Doug's answer. Doug's jaw looked dislocated.

"Sure—stay for dinner, Kovaks. We'll open some champagne. Go ahead, have that shower. There's time, isn't there, Doug?"

"Oodles." Doug mismanaged a smile.

Kovaks came to Dave and put a hand on the pocket of the terry-cloth robe. The hand was warm. "Cigarette?"

"On my dresser," Dave said. "Help yourself. Find clean clothes in there too." He sized Kovaks up. "I think my stuff will fit you. Anything at all."

Kovaks narrowed his long-lashed eyes, turned his head slightly away, worked his tongue skeptically behind closed lips. Then grinned and shrugged. "Okay—right, thanks." He walked out.

Doug said, "What are you up to?"

Dave picked up the pot in its carton. "I'll be down in the gallery for a little while," he said. "The packing room."

10

Ragged plastic pennants fluttered overhead—yellow, red, orange—on slack wires between corroded floodlight poles. Dave walked among secondhand cars toward a small wood-and-glass building in the weedy rear corner of a blacktop lot. PAT FARRELL GOOD USED CARS, the tin sign read. WE CARRY OUR OWN CONTRACTS. The cars were filmed with dust. Lettered on their windshields in chalky pink paint were false claims: LOW MILEAGE, CLEAN, FACTORY AIR, ALL POWER, STICK SHIFT, SHARP, even CHERRY—along with prices the dealer knew better than to expect.

Pat Farrell's was the kind of lot you walked onto with cash if you were smart. You chose what you wanted and didn't listen to why it was worth the three hundred fifty dollars it was marked. You pressed down on the upholstery, frowned under the hood, kicked the tires while the salesman followed you around, talking. Then you waved a hundred-dollar bill under his nose and drove out with twenty-five dollars' worth of scrap steel, cracked plastic, thin rubber, and the pink slip in your pocket.

At the foot of the plank stairs to the sales office was parked a European mini like the one that had died under Vern Taylor on the coast road yesterday morning. GAS SAVER was lettered on the glass. *Especially when it stalls,* Dave thought, and climbed the steps. The office door stood open because it was another hot morning. Inside, a man sat at a yellow wood desk whose top was covered by the spread-out classified ad pages of the *Examiner.* The man was circling ads with a felt-tip pen. His suit hung loose on him. A cigar was clenched in his teeth. An electric fan blew from the top of a tin file cabinet in a corner, ruffled his greenish toupee, chased the cigar smoke out through the glass louvers of a side window. He looked up, dropped the pen, laid the cigar on the desk edge, where earlier burns had made black fluting.

"Morning." He stood up, held out a hand. Where thick flesh must have padded out his cheeks once, a smile gathered back loose folds on either side of his mouth. The show of teeth was tobacco dingy. But the voice had warmth and a high gloss. "Pat Farrell. What can I do for you, sir?" Eyes like cheap green glass measured Dave and the smile died. "No—you don't want a car from me."

Dave laid a business card on the gray-print pages. It was the card Billy Wendell had given him day before yesterday. "When will he be in?"

"He won't be." Farrell dropped into his creaky swivel chair again. Above his head a flyspecked sign read YOUR CREDIT IS GOOD WITH US. "I fired him last week. That's not the way to put it. Makes me look bad. He fired himself. I warned him a dozen times, if he came on the lot drunk again, he had to go. But"—shoulder bones moved inside the bulky suit—"you feel sorry for them. Hell, Billy knows this business. He's good when he's sober."

"And when would that be?" Dave asked.

"Yeah." Farrell breathed a sour laugh. "Well, I just hoped the shock might help him. I hated to do it. He's old. Nobody else is going to take him on. Everybody in the business knows him. I was his last chance. And I put up with a lot for a long time. I'll take him back too. Told him so. If he'll quit the bottle. Nobody can do that for him. Man's got to do that for himself. Look at me." He put fingers inside his shirt collar to show how loose it was. "I know what I'm talking about. Not drink; no. Food. Loved to eat. Doc told me it was killing me. Either I lost a hundred pounds or I could plan on dropping dead here one of these days."

"You lost the weight," Dave said. "Congratulations."

Farrell wagged his head. "Haven't lost it all yet. That's why I'm wearing my old clothes. Looks like I borrowed this suit from somebody, doesn't it?" He plucked at an ample sleeve, laughed, picked up the cigar, clamped it in his teeth again. "I'm just waiting till I get down to one sixty-five. Then I'll buy new duds."

"I need Wendell's home address," Dave said.

"Don't think he's there." Farrell stood up again. "I went over there yesterday. To try to find out a little more about a contract he wrote that somebody skipped on. His landlady thinks he took a runout."

"She could check with his ex-wife," Dave said.

Farrell's eyebrows went up. "Never knew he had one. He never said anything about her."

"Their son died," Dave said. "He saw the notice in the paper. He hadn't known where they were, so he says. Close to forty years. He went to the funeral."

"Never mentioned them." Farrell opened a file drawer, brought a manila folder to the desk, sat down and copied an address on a note pad. He tore off the slip, pushed it across the open newspaper to Dave. "That's the dump where he was living. Always made me feel bad when I saw it. I mean, I was paying the man a decent wage. He didn't have to live like that."

"Liquor is expensive." Dave folded the paper and pushed it into a pocket. "Thank you."

"What's your interest in Billy?" Farrell followed Dave to the door. "You're not a cop. You're not a bill collector. What's your line?"

"Insurance," Dave said. "Death claims."

Farrell squinted. "Something wrong about the boy's death?"

"Everything." Dave started down the steps, turned. "Did Billy Wendell owe you money?"

Farrell turned down the corners of his mouth. "I advanced him twenty here, fifty there. Never kept count."

"You weren't pressing him hard for fifteen hundred dollars?"

The skin-crumpling smile again. It looked ghastly in the bright sunlight. "I'm good-hearted but I'm no fool. It's been thirty years since I let a drunk get into me for that kind of loot. No—maybe a hundred, two hundred at the outside. I kissed it goodbye when I gave it to him. You seen him?"

Lighting a cigarette, Dave nodded.

"Then you know a man wouldn't expect loans back from Billy Wendell. He'd work overtime for me when the wife and I had a date or went to Vegas for the weekend or whatever. I got it back that way—when he was sober enough to trust."

Dave gazed off across the dully glinting car tops, watched the anxious, frantic flutter of the little ragged flags, calling no one from the empty sun-stark boulevard beyond. "You thought I might be a bill collector. Why? Did they come around? Did they want you to garnishee his wages? Say for a bill like that. A thousand, fifteen hundred?"

"You telling me his son was murdered? For money?"

"Possibly." Dave shrugged. "Fifteen hundred is missing. Off his desk. He lay dead by the desk."

"Naw." Pat Farrell shook his head decisively. "He wouldn't kill anybody. Not Billy Wendell. He had his faults but he wouldn't kill anybody."

"He didn't need a large sum of money to stay out of jail?" Dave asked again. "Nobody was closing in on him?"

"Nobody knew he existed," Farrell said. Then he saw at the far corner of the lot a Mexican youth in a buttoned shirt without a tie, a fat brown girl carrying a baby in her arms, peering into a broad, low-slung maroon convertible with high tail fins and flashy hub caps. He bolted past Dave down the steps and, suit flapping, jogged across the tarmac, holding out his hand, grinning. His voice drifted back to Dave on the warm breeze. "Howdy. *Buenas días*. What can I do for you folks this beautiful morning? Isn't that a beauty? That's what I call a sharp automobile. And a steal at that price. An absolute steal."

The street was broad with a center divider where abandoned street-car rails turned to rust among dry weeds and clumps of sunflowers. Across the way, a chain-link fence with barbwire closed in vast gas storage tanks. Up the block, boxy stucco buildings made a corner—Lucky's bar and grill, the others empty, FOR RENT signs curling in the windows. Here, in the middle of the block, a red neon anchor and the word MOTEL tilted at the top of a steel post above a square of cement-block units painted clay color. Ivy geranium struggled in the hard dirt between a cracked sidewalk and the small-windowed walls. Blacktop covered the inner courtyard, where a greasy motorcycle stood with pieces of itself scattered around its wheels and there was an automobile that would have discouraged even Pat Farrell.

Spiky upthrusts of tired Spanish bayonet guarded the car entrance. A red-and-white sign beside a Dutch door on the cabin to the left said HI! RING BELL FOR SERVICE. He rang bell and a cat came from somewhere and rubbed its yellow stripes against his legs. He crouched and scratched its ears. It purred. The top of the Dutch door opened and a knobby-jawed woman gave him a smile. She wore a crisscross halter and shorts of a Hawaiian material whose hibiscuses had faded many voyages ago. There was nothing Hawaiian about her look or her talk. They were strictly Little Rock, Arkansas.

"We got lots of room," she said. She rattled up a clipboard on a chain from inside and laid it on top of the lower shelf. There was a ballpoint pen on a braided nylon cord. "Take your choice."

"I'm looking for Billy Wendell." Dave handed her his Medallion card. "Unit nine, someone told me."

"That's right." She opened the lower half of the door and stepped out. Her skin in the sun was dead white. She was all elbows, knees, collarbones. "But he's not in it. Hasn't been here two, three days. I don't expect him. You gonna find him? Cause when you do, remind him he owes me three weeks' rent. Place is nigh empty. I got to eat too, tell him."

"Isn't this your good season?" Dave asked.

"I don't have a good season," she said.

"Can I see his room?" Dave asked. "Before the police?"

"Police!" She gawked. "What's he done?"

"A member of his family met with an accident," Dave said. "That person was insured by my company. We have a set investigative routine, you know?" He gave her a smile. "All right? Or is the room rented?"

"Fat chance. Here." She reached inside the door, where keys jingled. "Nope. Forgot. Maid's got it. Cleanin' up today. Look for her." She turned her head, sniffed. "Damn! I boiled that coffee." She vanished back inside. The cat jumped up on the shelf, knocked down the clipboard, followed her.

Next to the door of nine stood a square canvas

laundry hamper on wheels. Sheets draggled from it. The door was open and inside the room a vacuum whined. He peered in. A shadowy female with a white cloth tied over her hair sullenly pushed furniture. Dave stepped inside. The maid was black and young. She didn't appear even to glance at him but she said, "Ain' ready yet."

Closet doors stood open on emptiness. Big shabby slacks and jackets lay across a grudging upholstered chair with greasy arms. Hats, a worn raincoat, two pairs of cracked shoes. Dave picked up and dropped a tangle of stained neckties. "Did he leave anything else?"

"You the Man?" She glanced at him this time but without much interest. "Ain' been through the drawers yet." She jerked her head at a brown-painted thrift-shop chest under a wavery mirror. Dave found underwear and socks, empty bourbon bottles with supermarket labels, candy-bar wrappers, a cellophane bag with three dried-out doughnuts, moldy bread in white wax paper. He shut the drawers. "Nothing else?"

"Wastebasket out there." She ran the shiny tube of the vacuum over faded plaid window curtains that matched the spread on the sagging bed. "He dead or somethin'?"

"Or something," Dave said. In the morning sun glare he squatted by the wastebasket—cardboard papered in plaid—and lifted out another whiskey bottle and a cigarette carton. Under these was a folded section of newspaper. He put on his glasses and looked it over. Circled in red pencil was the story of Rick Wendell's murder. The page number was 17 and Billy hadn't lied—the address of the canyon house was there. Dave tore off the sheet, folded it, pocketed it, took a second newspaper section from the basket.

This wasn't from the *Times*. It was from a local advertising throwaway. And there was a spread on the Mr. Marvelous contest to come, with pictures of, among others, Rick Wendell. He and Ace Kegan flanked Bobby Reich, who wore the little white shorts. A lot of other men were in the pictures—owners, contestants, most of whom Dave had met on his tour of the bars. Captions identified them and named their places of business. The text didn't say what kind of businesses they were—this was a family paper. It was dated a week ahead of the murder. So Billy had lied about one thing—he'd known his son was alive and well and where to find him. Dave tore off this sheet and pushed it in with the other one.

The wastebasket held another bottle, a pizza tin gummy with sauce, wadded paper napkins, a waxed cup with the Coca-Cola trademark—and then the torn-up pieces of a letter. Dave fitted the ragged edges together on the gritty blacktop. *My Dear Son— you will have forgotten me and no wonder since your mother and I came to a parting of the ways years ago but I want to say how proud I am to read in the paper that you are a success in life even though your father has not* . . . The writing, sprawling and unsteady, broke off there.

Dave tucked the fragments into the pocket with

the news sheets and poked into the wastebasket again. A half-eaten hamburger in its gold-foil Jack in the Box wrapper, a corn chip bag, last week's *TV Guide*. And that was all. Dave dumped the trash back into the basket, got to his feet, brushing his hands together. He called thanks to the vacuuming girl and walked back to the motel office, where the bony woman leaned on the lower half of the Dutch door, drinking coffee from a mug with the yellow round "Smile" face on it, and eating a pastry.

Dave asked, "He had a home away from home—right?"

She nodded. "Lucky's," she said. "Right up at the corner. You can't miss it."

A glass-and-steel phone booth waited beside the Spanish bayonets. He stepped into it, dragged the phone book on its chain from under the little corner shelf and thumbed the gritty pages. The yellow ones. He found the listing. *Hang Ten*. It had a red pencil mark around it, like the mark around the story of Rick Wendell's death in the paper. He dropped the directory on its chain and got into the Electra. The radio went on with the ignition. A Beethoven quartet, one of the Rasoumovskys, he thought. He sat and listened to it for a minute before he let the brake go and rolled along the block to the lonely buildings huddled on the corner in the sun.

Out the open door of Lucky's came an eye-stinging smell of pine disinfectant. Inside, someone short and fat, cocooned in a big white apron, mopped a floor of worn black vinyl tile. Like big metal insects stunned by the smell, stools stood legs up on the bar, chairs on little tables. There was a big metal bucket with rubber rollers on top. When the stubby being dropped the drizzly gray strings of the mop between these, levered them closed and pulled, there was loud squealing. Dave coughed. The mop wielder turned. The face was round, white, withered, like an apple forgotten in a cellar.

"You're just a shade early for a drink."

"I don't need a drink," Dave said. "I'm an insurance investigator and I've got a question or two about one of your regulars. Billy Wendell."

"Insurance?" The popping of dirty soap bubbles was audible in the hush. "That mean he's dead?"

"Do they die a lot?" Dave wondered.

"They're not young, most of 'em." The mopping began again. Cigarette butts fled from side to side. "Billy hasn't been around last couple nights was why I asked."

"He's not dead," Dave said.

"Gone off to find his wife and kid, then." The mop went into the bucket again. The cigarette butts drowned. "I didn't think he'd have the nerve. They talk like that, you know. Daydreams, drink dreams. I've got customers been planning to break out, change their lives, for years. Never do it. Truth. Most of 'em. Never did do nothin', never will. I only know two kinds of people in this life—them that make things happen, them that things happen to." The mop went to work again.

"And Billy Wendell?" Dave asked.

"He'd been talking about his son. Read a piece

in the paper about him, how he's got his own business." Chunky elbows bent and straightened. "Billy
was proud of him. Success, he says. Not a failure
like his old man." Dave backed from the wet sweep
of the mop and the little figure bowed into sunlight
from the door. The voice hadn't let him be sure of
it, but he decided now that she was female, a fat
little woman of fifty in men's clothes, with a man's
haircut. "When he got fired from the used car lot,
Billy says it was okay with him. He could go back
to his son, his son would look after him, his son
wouldn't let his old man go down to destruction."

"Billy was here every night?"

"About. Oh, he'd get economy spells. Scuse me."
She nodded and Dave stepped out onto the sidewalk
while the mop spread dirty suds across the doorsill.
The woman leaned the mop against the door, wiped
fat little hands on the wraparound apron, stepped
out blinking into the sun. "There'd be a night or
two he'd drink in his motel room." A stubby thumb
jerked in the direction of the cinder-block buildings
under the neon anchor up the weedy block. "But
he'd miss the company. We'd miss him too. It gets
like a family, place like this. So he'd soon be back.
TV's poor company, you know. Nothin' to drinkin'
alone."

"Monday night," Dave said. "Was that one of the
times he tried TV?"

"Monday?" She looked back into the dark bar as
if the answer might come from there. Then she
looked at him again and her face puckered into a
grin. "Naw, not Monday. Hell, we had a celebration

Monday. Birthday party. For Lilian. Lilian Drill and her old man. They been coming in here must be five, six years. Lilian's just the most fun. Everybody loves Lilian. No—Billy was here till two, till closing. All the regulars was here. Billy especially. They're a set, him and Lilian."

"How's that?" Dave asked.

"The Beautiful People," the pudgy woman said. "You heard that expression. Naw, I don't mean these days, but once. Lilian was in pictures in the thirties. And Billy—everybody's seen his photos, polo playing, horse shows, yachts. He was handsome. Money, high life. Yup, him and Lilian. They're a set."

"What time did he get here Monday? Late?"

"Five in the afternoon. He built sandwiches while I frosted the cake. I always bake the cakes myself. Store bought, they're sawdust. Baked it, decorated it myself. My old man was a baker. Before he decided there was more money in booze." She poked inside the apron and brought out a crushed pack of cigarettes. She lit one with a paper match and blew the smoke at the sidewalk. She wore tennis shoes, child size. "Thing he couldn't remember was the booze was for the customers. Killed him. Anyway, I decorated the cake." She gestured in the air. "*Lucky's Own Movie Queen*—that's what I wrote on it." She gave a little sad laugh and shook her head. "Lilian cried."

I I

Dwayne Huncie said, "I don't need no lawyer. I *am* a lawyer." He wore new cowboy boots, the tooling dyed deep reds and purples. His pants were striped and sharply creased. His belt served as a sling for his pink-satin-shirted belly. It was a new belt with a wrought silver buckle the size of a pack of playing cards. He stood, big and bow-legged and blinking under a crimped-brim straw cowboy hat in Yoshiba's night office, two uniformed California highway patrolmen, guns on hips, guarding the door behind him. "I can handle this."

"You *were* a lawyer," Yoshiba said, "but that was in Texas and some time ago." He leafed over a Xeroxed record file. "You were disbarred in 1957. For bribing jurors. You served time for it." He sat back, laid a hand on the file, blinked through the desk light. "You served time pretty often. Didn't anybody ever tell you the man who acts as his own lawyer has a fool for a client?"

"Man don't need no lawyer that tells the simple truth." Huncie shifted a lump of tobacco from one whiskery cheek to the other, nodded, eyeing a chair. "Can I set down? That was kind of a long ride from Saugus."

"Help yourself," Yoshiba said. "You understand that this is serious? A case of murder?"

"I didn't figure you'd have every lawman in the state scourin' nickel and dime trailer camps to haul me back here just for pissin' in some alley. But you got the wrong man. I never killed nobody." He dropped his loose bulk onto a hard chair. "Who is it's dead?"

"Richard William Wendell," Yoshiba said.

From a corner, a deputy district attorney in Levi's and a Little League cap asked, "Know the name?"

"Heard of it." Huncie jerked a nod.

"We've got a suspect locked up," Yoshiba said. "Lawrence Henry Johns. You know that name too, right? Right. The mother of the victim found Johns standing over the body cleaning off the gun the victim was shot with."

"Well, almighty Gawd," Huncie said moderately. "Ain't that enough?"

"It's a little too much," Dave said. He leaned on a file cabinet, nursing a paper cup of coffee and smoking. "The only fingerprints on the weapon belong to the mother. There are powder burns on the hand and chest of the deceased, whose gun it was. And fifteen hundred dollars is missing from his desk."

"Oh?" Huncie said. "Who are you?"

Dave told him. Wind that smelled of warm night ocean breathed in at the open window next to him. "No one else can account for that fifteen hundred. We have an idea you can."

"Me?" Huncie tried for a laugh but it broke and

there was fear in his watery blue eyes. "How the hell did you scrounge up that idea, will you tell me?"

Yoshiba looked at the armed men. "Open that door, will you, and tell them to send in the witness?"

Jomay Johns was blond and scrubbed as a child. But her jeans and blouse were grubby. She didn't look more than twelve. Her hair was a baroque complex of yellow upsweeps and downfalls. "You son of a bitch," she said to Huncie. "You run off and left me without no clothes or nothin'. Me and BB. Plus, you stole that money. You dirty old bastard. You didn't just steal it. You stole it twice!"

Huncie eyed her and shifted the chaw again. "Where did you get to? I left you and BB gettin' malts and French fries at that there McDonald's and when I come back, you was noplace to be seen."

"You're a liar," she said. "You drove off in the camper. When you didn't come for your food, I went out in the lot and looked. Wasn't no camper there. I had seventeen dollars change and didn't know nobody in town."

Huncie spread big hands. "I discovered I didn't have no more tobacco. I went lookin' for some. This here ain't chewin' tobacco country, sweetheart. I had one hell of a time. Then I come back and you're gone."

"Bullshit," she said. "Bullshit." She looked, outraged, from one to another of the shadowy figures in the office. "Do you believe this old bullshitter?"

"Take it easy," Yoshiba told her. "Larson, give her a chair, will you? Sit down, Mrs. Johns." While the Little League D.A. got up and fumbled in the crowded half dark, getting the chair out of the corner, Yoshiba said to Huncie, "This witness says you had in your possession at eleven o'clock Monday night a large bundle of twenty-dollar bills."

"I had 'em," Huncie said.

"Where did you get them?"

"They was owin' and I collected 'em," Huncie said.

"Owing," Yoshiba said, "to whom? For what?"

Back of him, propped against the window ledge, the public defender, Khazoyan, in a black mohair suit and a ruffled shirtfront, yawned noisily.

Huncie squinted at him past the glare of the desk lamp. "We can get this over with quick and let that man get home to bed," he said. "I got 'em off the desk in that little house next to the big house up there on Pinyon Trail in that canyon—house belonging to, way I understood it, this here Wendell, the fella which her little runaway husband"—he nodded at dim Jomay—"the one you call Lawrence Henry Johns, says he was going to get the money from he owed."

"Just as simple as that," Yoshiba said.

Huncie nodded, rose, creaked in the new boots to the window. Khazoyan stepped aside. Huncie spat a long brown stream of tobacco juice into the night. Wiping his mouth with a hand, he turned back. "Just as simple as that. Not a dead body in it. Larry was to collect the money and I was to drive out to that barny-lookin' place on the beach and get it off him next mornin'. Hell, I saved him and me both trouble, that was all. You too, Jomay honey.

If you'd only kept your pretty little ass on that there plastic stool in McDonald's."

"I don't think you're a trouble saver," Yoshiba said. "I think you're a trouble maker, and I bet I'm not the first person who's told you that. How did you find Wendell's? Did you follow him and Johns up there?"

"Nope." With a sigh, the big old man dropped onto his chair again. "First I figured to call in on him at his place of business, but time I got her and BB into a movie she was half willin' to see—you think combin' and fixin' all that pretty yella hair don't take time, you ain't lived much with women—I got there too late. There was some sissy boy back of the bar and I asked him. Wendell had left. So—I looked up Wendell in the phone book and took me a little drive up there. Nice night for it."

"I thought you wanted us to get to bed," Khazoyan complained. "You want to cut to the good part?"

"All right," Huncie said agreeably. "I got up there and seen 'em through the window, standin' by the desk. Wendell took this envelope out of his jacket and tore it open and took out these bundles of bills and showed 'em to Larry. They left the room. I stepped in, picked the money up off the desk, stepped out again. There it is, all of it, the plain and simple truth. Not only wasn't there no murder in it; there wasn't no theft, neither. Ask her—don't he owe you that money, Jomay?"

"Not anymore," she said. "You do."

"Hold on," Yoshiba said. "Johns says they heard you. Wendell came out, there was an argument and

a struggle and a gun went off. You didn't walk out
of there with that money. Not till Wendell had pulled
a gun on you and you'd wrestled with him and it
had gone off and killed him. Then you left. But I'll
bet it wasn't at a walk."

"It was," Huncie said. "And nobody come out of
that other room. The door stayed shut." He tilted
the straw hat back, tilted the chair back, ran a thick
finger along the stubbly edge of his tobacco-working
jaw. "But somebody did run."

"Somebody?" Khazoyan made a waking-up sound.

Huncie looked at him. "Sure. You didn't think I'd
open up and tell you all this if I didn't think I had
some chance of provin' it, do you? There was a
witness. I seen him runnin' away, up the back there."

Yoshiba picked up a pen. "Description?"

"Aw, now, Lieutenant—you know better'n that.
It was pitch dark up there. Big pines all around."

"But you did say 'him,'" Yoshiba said. "You know
it was a man." He glanced back and up at Dave.

Huncie said, "Well, no. Now that you mention it,
guess I don't." Scowling to himself, he let the chair
legs down with a clack, got up and went to the
window again to spit. "Could have been a she-male.
Did have a big handbag, the kind they wear on a
strap over their shoulder. Seen it bangin' against
her hip when she run off through the trees. Her,
him."

"You didn't follow?" Dave asked.

"What for? I had what I come for, purely legal.
But I can give you a lead." He paused, chewing,
watching their faces. "When I got down to the

camper, there was another car parked there. One of them fancy pickups, you know? Look more like a sports car than a truck?"

"El Camino," Yoshiba said.

"That's it. Was a truck, though. Little name lettered real modest on the door—Thomas Owens, AIA. My Lord! Why, that's the name of that fella Larry was eatin' off of in that beach place, ain't it? Owens?"

"What does this mean?" Gail Ewing blocked the doorway. Far down the room at her back, light from a wicker-shaded swag lamp islanded the grouped furniture by the hooded fireplace and made black mirrors of the tall glass wall panels. She wore a housecoat and no makeup. Her eyelids were swollen, her speech thick. She pushed at rumpled hair. "Do you realize what time it is?"

On the deck, the dark dunes at their back, Yoshiba, Khazoyan, Larson and Dave watched sea wind play with the long yellow hair of Jomay Johns, who had pressed the bell push. Yoshiba held his wallet above the girl's head, let it fall open. "Police," he said. "Like to come in and talk to you a few minutes."

"No, not tonight." Gail Ewing backed, started to shut the door. "There's an invalid in the house. Everyone else is asleep. I've taken a sleeping pill myself, and I simply wouldn't be—"

"Sorry, Mrs. Ewing, but it can't wait." Yoshiba put square, thick hands on the Johns girl's little shoulders and pushed her ahead of him into the room. Gail Ewing was forced to back up. Yoshiba moved in. Larson and Khazoyan followed. And

Dave. Gail Ewing narrowed the yellow eyes at him.

"You!" she said. "You're responsible for this."

"You know better than that," Dave said. "If anyone's responsible, it's you. If you'd gone to your brother with Larry's problem, he'd have given the boy the money he needed, or gotten him a lawyer, done what was necessary. None of the rest of it would have happened."

"I refuse to believe that." Her chin thrust out stubbornly. She turned to the squat policeman. "Lieutenant Yoshiba, I've told you my brother's an invalid. He's not to be disturbed."

"I don't think we'll have to disturb him." Yoshiba shut the door quietly, firmly. "You can probably answer our questions."

"I don't have to." She clutched the robe at her throat. "I'm entitled to an attorney."

Yoshiba's eyebrows rose a fraction of an inch. "You're not charged with anything."

Larson stepped forward, taking off his Little League cap. He was going bald under it. "I'm George Larson, Mrs. Ewing—deputy district attorney. This is Art Khazoyan. He's an attorney also—public defender's office. We'll see that your rights are protected in every way."

Her mouth twitched but she didn't answer him. She turned her anger on the little blond girl. "What are you doing back here? Haven't you caused enough trouble?"

"Mother! Are you out of your mind?" Trudy's voice came from the shadowy top of the wooden bird-flight stairs. She was a slim silhouette, something bulky in her arms. Down the high gallery behind her, light made a yellow rectangle of a doorway. "She's come back for her baby."

"Oh, God." Gail Ewing shut her eyes, rubbed her forehead.

"For Christ sake!" Mark Dimond was a jerky shadow in the lighted doorway, kicking into pants. He came fast along the gallery, buttoning his fly, to stand beside Trudy. "Tom wants her to stay here, anyhow. You know that."

"It's the damn sleeping pill!" Gail Ewing shouted at him. "I loathe the things. I wouldn't have taken one if it weren't for all this—" She finished the sentence with a frantic flipping of her hands. She said to Jomay, "Go along, child—I'm sorry."

Jomay glared sourly at her and went for the stairs. Trudy called down to her. "It's all right. She slept all the time you were gone." Jomay climbed the stairs.

Yoshiba told Gail Ewing, "What we need to know is about Mr. Owens's car—the El Camino, the one parked up in the port now. Who drove it Monday night? He didn't."

"With two broken legs?" Her tone scathed him. "Your powers of deduction are amazing, Lieutenant."

"Sarcasm is wasted on Orientals, Mrs. Ewing," Yoshiba said. "We're extremely impassive. Slights and abuse run off our backs like water off a duck—a mandarin duck, of course."

"Forgive me," she said stiffly. "I don't know anything about the car. I was at a City Council meeting that night. I drove my own car."

"I thought Trudy smashed up your car," Dave said.

"I have a replacement," Gail Ewing said. "Thanks to Sequoia Accident and Indemnity Corporation, Mr. Brandstetter." She smiled coldly. "Insurance, remember?"

Larson said, "On halting offshore oil drilling."

"What?" Yoshiba looked at him.

"That was what the City Council session was about," Larson said. "I was there myself. I saw Mrs. Ewing."

She studied him, nodded. "Yes. That's right."

"So who had the car?" Yoshiba asked again.

"No one," she said.

"Mark Dimond," Dave said. He looked up the stairs. The boy wasn't standing beside the girls and the baby anymore. Dave started to turn for the door. Yoshiba stopped him. "Don't sweat it. They're out there." He meant two uniformed officers who had followed them up the dark coast road in a patrol car.

"Who's out there?" Gail Ewing asked sharply and tried to push past them to the door.

Someplace out of sight and half out of hearing, the dogs began to bark.

"Take it easy, Mrs. Ewing." Yoshiba stepped in front of her. "We just want to talk to the boy."

"What do you *mean!*" Trudy came down the stairs at a run. She was barefoot again, in the same gray bells and appliquéd shirt, breasts showing firm through the thin cloth. She didn't wear the sunglasses tonight, though, and the bruises around her eyes, along with the missing teeth, made her young face an old mask. "Talk to him about what? He didn't do anything. He couldn't!"

"He wasn't here Monday night," Dave said. "Your uncle said you were alone in the house with him when Larry turned up missing. Where was Mark?"

She said defiantly, "He went to see a man in the Audio-Visual Department at UCLA. Someone he had a letter of introduction to from his department head. He'd been putting it off. That night he decided to go and get it over with."

"And not take you?" Dave asked.

"I had to be here." She explained it to him as to a little child. "To look after Tom."

The door swung inward. They all looked at the black oblong. Sea wind came in and so did two uniformed men holding Mark Dimond by the arms between them. He was bare-chested, barefoot. "He was going to take off, Lieutenant. In the El Camino."

"Let go of him!" Trudy flung herself at them.

Yoshiba caught her. "Easy," he said. "It's going to be all right. We just want to ask him a couple of simple questions."

Trudy stared frightened past the lieutenant's bulky shoulder at the boy with the helmet of black hair. She was asking her own questions. Not aloud. With her eyes.

Larson said, "You were up at the Wendell house on Monday night, weren't you?"

Dimond was very pale. "I don't get this," he said. "I don't get this at all." He squinted, twisted his face. "What house?"

"Wendell. He was killed that night, remember?" Yoshiba said. "A kid who lived here, kid by the name of Larry Johns, is being held for his murder. Does that clear it up for you?"

"Oh, Christ," Dimond breathed. His eyes were on Trudy's face. They seemed to plead.

"So you do know who I'm talking about?" Yoshiba asked.

Dimond tried a mystified laugh. "What would I be doing up there? I went to UCLA that night."

"Is that right? Did you see the man you had the letter of introduction to? What's his name?"

Something went out of Dimond's face. "He wasn't there. Nobody was there. But that doesn't mean—"

"Somebody was at Wendell's," Yoshiba said. "He tells us a pickup with the name Thomas Owens on the door was parked at the foot of the stairs. By the mailboxes. On Pinyon Trail. Mrs. Ewing, here, didn't drive the car. Mr. Owens didn't drive it. He told Brandstetter his niece was here with him that night. She says you weren't. And you do have a key to that car. That's the key, there, in your hand, isn't it?"

"I want a lawyer," Mark Dimond said.

"Mark!" Gail Ewing gasped. "Oh, my God!" She was very white. She caught at Larson's arm. He steadied her. Mark Dimond watched her, bewildered.

"What's wrong with you? You hated Larry Johns as much as I did. More."

"Oh, but, Mark—the death of an innocent man—"

"What! What the hell are you saying?" Dimond

struggled in the grip of the officers. "Now, wait— wait just a fucking minute, Gail. I didn't kill anyone." He looked wildly from Yoshiba to Larson to Khazoyan to Dave. "I never said that. I didn't, I didn't!"

"He didn't," Trudy said. "He couldn't have."

"Fine," Yoshiba said. "So what were you doing there?"

Dimond sulked. "I want a lawyer."

"I think I can tell you what he was doing there," Dave said. "He followed Larry Johns. And he took along his trusty tape recorder. It's a portable, hangs in a case on a shoulder strap. That was what Dwayne Huncie mistook for a woman's handbag when he saw him running off through the trees."

"That how it was?" Yoshiba asked Dimond.

Sick, the boy turned his head. After a moment's disgusted silence he drew breath, let it out and said wearily, "Yeah. I'd brought the dogs inside. There's a room for them at the back, under the carport. And I heard Larry on the kitchen phone. Asking for money. Agreeing to meet this Rick on the coast road, eight that night. It proved what I knew he was." He looked at Trudy. "A hustler. The kind that peddles sex to perverts."

"You're eating Tom Owens's food," Dave told him. "Sleeping under his roof. That's a hell of a word."

The dark boy flushed. "Okay. Homosexuals, gays—whatever you want. I'm sorry." He looked at Trudy again. "I told you, but you wouldn't believe me. He was so sweet, he'd had such a lousy life. I had to prove to you what he was. So"—he faced Yoshiba again—"I took my recorder and stood outside Wendell's windows and I got a tape."

"Mark!" Trudy said. "You didn't! That's revolting. Sneaking, spying. What *are* you?"

"In love with you, dummy." Mark struggled to break from the officers again. He said to Yoshiba, "I've still got it. I kept it. Didn't play it for Trudy because after that night Larry was gone anyway. If you'll let me, I'll get it and you can hear it. You'll love it, Trudy. You'll really love your fair-haired cracker when you hear that tape."

Yoshiba said, "Go with him, Ramirez."

Minutes later, the tape recorder, black leather case laid open like the lid of a coffin, stood on the big low deal table under the light, its five-inch reels of clear plastic winking as they turned. Gail Ewing sat stone-faced on the long wicker couch, Trudy next to her, biting her nails, watching Mark, who stood over the machine. Yoshiba and Dave flanked him. Larson and Khazoyan stood at the end of the table. The uniformed officers leaned by the front door. Jomay Johns sat in the dark at the top of the stairs with BB asleep in her lap. Their hair glowed like that of angels in a painting darkened by centuries of soot. Dave wished he had a drink.

The tape stopped hissing to itself. Distances of crickets skirred. There was the far, lost drone of a jet plane. A voice deep and rumbling that still managed to have something feminine about it said, *It's in here, safe and sound. I haven't even opened it.*

Fifteen hundred dollars in small bills. Wasn't that what you said? Paper rattled and tore. *See? There. Do you want to count it? Go ahead, count it if you want to.* Another rattle of paper.

Aw, Rick, I don't want to count it, man. This was Larry Johns's voice, hard and echoey in the room. *And look, I'll pay it back. I promise. I mean it.* There was a knocking sound. Perhaps a shoe had kicked a desk leg. Wendell's voice again above a rustling whisper of cloth: *Oh, Larry, no. It's my gift. You don't know what it means to have you come back. How I've dreamed, hoped, wished, prayed. When you phoned today, I cried, I really cried with happiness. I—*

Larry Johns's voice cut across Wendell's. *No, I don't take money for sex, Rick. It's a loan, man. I'll get a gig and pay you back. Otherwise—*

All right, Larry, all right. Now just let me hold you. Oh, God. A long silence. A low moaning. Then a whispered, *Now, Larry? Please—now? Yes, in here. Yes, yes.* A latch rattled, a door swung, brushing carpet, hinges squeaking slightly. A door closed. The crickets went on with their shrill plaintive pulsing. There was a scuff of shoe leather on cement, a crackling of leaves under soles. The tape clicked. The empty hissing started again. Mark Dimond leaned, reached, punched a plastic key. The reels halted.

Yoshiba stood frowning for a moment in the sea-sighing silence, then touched the machine with a shoe. "They don't exactly beat the camera, do they? What went with the dialogue?"

Dimond flushed darkly, shifted his feet, rubbed his smooth brown chest. "Well—he, uh, took the envelope out of his jacket. He tore it open and took out packs of bills. He tried to give them to Larry but he wouldn't touch them. So the big stud, Wendell—he, like, thumbed the edges, you know? As if to show Larry the bread was all there or something—right?" The dark boy gestured uneasily. "What do you want me to say? I mean, okay, he dropped the envelope and money on the desk and—" Dimond glanced unhappily at Gail and Trudy on the couch, up into the dimness where Jomay sat silent. "Well, it was kind of freaky to watch, you know? Made me feel a little nauseated. I mean, he started running his hands over Larry. Like he was a girl. Wow! Through his hair and all that." Dimond looked at the floor, blew air out through his nostrils, mumbled, "Held his head, tipped it back, you know, and kissed him on the mouth. Took him in his arms, you know?" Dimond looked up. "Hell, Lieutenant, I don't want to—"

"Yeah, okay, kid. They went into the other room?"

"Right. And I was relieved when they did."

"And you left, did you?" Dave wondered.

"I wanted to but the windows on that other room were open too because it was a hot night. I knew I ought to go there if I was going to get real proof for Trudy. And I took a step in that direction when I see the door from outside open and this lifelike, inflatable Gabby Hayes pokes his head in. Whiskers, chewing tobacco—you could smell stockyards twenty feet off. He takes a quick look around, walks straight to the desk, picks up the bread, and walks out with it. Wow! I didn't know what to do. I couldn't do anything, could I? I mean, I was in a very ridiculous position."

"That wouldn't be my word," Dave said.

"It was contemptible." Trudy sprang up and walked into the dark. "Disgusting. It makes me sick."

Yoshiba said, "So you ran, did you?"

Dimond was looking worriedly after Trudy. "What? Yeah, I ran. Waited up in the trees till I heard his truck drive off down the road. Then I got out of there."

Yoshiba looked at Larson. "I want to book him on failure to report a felony."

Larson glanced at the beautiful expensive room. "He'd be out on O.R. tomorrow morning." He put the Little League cap on again. "Waste of time."

"Nobody saw him leave," Yoshiba said.

"Ho," Larson said. "You want to book him for the murder? You'd have to let Johns out, then."

Khazoyan said, "That sounds good to me."

"Forget it," Yoshiba said.

"I should think so," Gail Ewing said indignantly.

"Just don't go anywhere," Yoshiba told Mark Dimond.

12

Below Pinyon Trail, at the foot of a fern slope where a summer-scant creek threaded among moss-rusty boulders, deer lay in the morning shadows of the pines. Three of them. When Yoshiba drove the unmarked Los Santos Police Department car past above them, they didn't get up. They only raised their heads, swiveled big soft ears. Their eyes were wide and calm.

"Will you look at that?" Yoshiba said. "What are we—twenty miles from downtown L.A.?"

"If that," Dave said. "We forget—the interloper is man. Hold it. This is the place."

Three cars crowded the patch of yellow dirt in front of tin mailboxes on paint-chalky posts. One car had the high rear fender fins of the fifties. That would be Billy Wendell's. One was a station wagon, a broad one from the sixties, the tailgate down, weighted with baled alfalfa. Heather's, of course. The third was a VW with a cloth top. Rick's. Dave had seen it here the other morning. Was she going to let the weeds and creepers have it? Yoshiba slowed but didn't stop.

"What's on up the trail?" he asked.

"I'm told it makes a loop," Dave said.

Yoshiba moved the lever to "L" and put a square foot on the accelerator pedal. The car climbed a wide, bumpy half circle in the cool shadows of the pines. At the top, where Heather Wendell's ruined blacktop driveway raked downward from the trail, he braked the car, killed the engine. In the sudden quiet, a quail called. Yoshiba opened his door and stepped out. Dave did the same. Yoshiba nodded to where gray wood shingling showed through the trees below.

"That's the place."

"Garage," Dave said, "where she stables her horses." He shifted ground. "Here. From here you can see part of the house, farther down."

Yoshiba came, looked, grunted. His blunt shoetip nudged the dust of the road edge where footprints showed. "Looks like somebody waited around up here. Deck shoes. New ones. Kegan?"

"Probably." Dave checked his watch. "We'd better catch her before she gets out on those horses. There's country up here where you can't follow by automobile."

But Yoshiba was crouching. "Two cars were parked here lately. Look. Different sets of tires, side by side. Both small cars. This one"—a short, thick finger made a circle in the air above a dark patch soaked into the dust—"had a bad oil leak."

Dave glanced around. Across the road a hill climbed to a crest maybe thirty feet above. A few dying pines but mostly scrub and rock. Nothing was built there, nothing to the left or to the right. Only below. "It could be a place where kids park to make out."

"Almost have to be." Yoshiba grunted, got to his feet. "Let's go down this way."

At the foot of the drive, beside the garage-cum-stable, Heather Wendell and her gaunt husband sat horses, she the little paint mare *(Buffy doesn't like men)* and he the sorrel gelding. The woman wore a plaid shirt, jeans, a black charro hat; the man Levi's pants and jacket stitched for someone bulkier—his son, no doubt. A bowl-brimmed straw sombrero shaded his long, rutted face. The horse hoofs moved noiselessly on the pine needle cushion of the yard. The man and woman drew rein and stared.

"What is it?" Heather Wendell asked Yoshiba. "I told you to keep him"—she jerked an angry nod at Dave—"away from here."

"You don't want to be ungrateful," Yoshiba said. "He got you back quite a chunk of money you'd never have seen again. Close to twelve hundred dollars."

She sat up straight, blinking puzzlement.

"From that brown bank envelope on Rick's desk," Dave said. "Remember? You let me take it away the other morning, with the wrapper tabs, each marked five hundred dollars. A check with the bank showed Rick had withdrawn that amount Monday afternoon."

"What for?" she said.

"Rick had promised it to Larry Johns. On the telephone at noon. You picked up the phone for that call. He told you his name. But you made out to me you'd never heard it until that night."

Her mouth twitched. "I'd forgotten."

"Come on now, Mrs. Wendell," Yoshiba said.

"Now, look here!" Billy Wendell tried to make himself sound ominous. He shifted in the saddle, kicking a foot free of its stirrup, as if he were going to dismount. But he didn't. He finished lamely, "I don't like your tone."

"It's possible the name didn't mean anything to you at that point," Dave said. "Johns says he was up here before with your son. A few weeks ago. But it was after the bar closed. You told me your hours differed, so maybe you didn't know about it. But if you did and then Larry Johns turned up again, you'd have had reason to suspect he represented the same threat to you other boys had done—Monkey, Savage."

She paled and seemed to sag in the saddle.

"You're guessing," Billy Wendell blustered.

"Based on this," Dave said. "That your wife and Ace Kegan had a conference Monday night." He looked at Heather. "You didn't go to that horse film as you told me. You went to the Chardash restaurant next to the theater and talked the situation over with Ace. He'd had a phone call where Larry Johns gave his name too. And you both knew it spelled trouble. Possibly disaster. That was why neither of you ate."

She touched dry lips with a dry tongue.

"Then you drove up here," Yoshiba said. "To try to stop the thing before it could get under way. Your son didn't like being interrupted and browbeaten and he went for his gun to run you off. Kegan rushed him and your son ended up dead. Wasn't that how it was?"

148

"No!" she said loudly. "Ace wasn't even here. He has a dreadful temper. It was still under control when he got into his car in the theater parking lot but by the time he got up here to the house, he'd worked himself into a fury. He said if Rick didn't listen to reason, he'd beat it into him. And he could do it. He was a prize fighter. His fists are like hammers. Yes, I know Rick was bigger, but he hadn't any fight in him."

"He had the gun," Dave reminded her.

"The gun never came into it." Heather swung out of the saddle. The stocky little horse took a step backward, shaking her head, clinking bridle fastenings. "Because Ace didn't see Rick that night. He was raving. I won't repeat what he said he'd do to that boy."

"Raving," Dave said. "But you made him go?"

"It wasn't easy but he respects me and finally through his rage he heard me. He knew what had happened before. He's very nearly gone to prison for beating people. And he'd be heartsick afterward if he hurt Rick. They were very close."

"And he left?" Yoshiba asked.

"With bad grace," she said, "but yes, he left. I watched him get into his car and start it before I went on up the stairs."

"What about this twelve hundred dollars?" Billy Wendell's big hand smoothed the sorrel's mane. "Have you got it with you?"

"It's evidence," Yoshiba said. "The court will hold it till the man who stole it is tried."

"Who was he?"

Dave told the story of Dwayne Huncie.

Yoshiba said, "It's too bad about the three hundred. Especially when you see the clothes he got himself with it—if you could call them clothes. But the balance—once the trial's over, it'll be released to you. I don't know how soon that will be."

"What do they need with it?" Billy Wendell asked. "The bank won't have a record. Not if the bills were only twenties. They don't record them unless they're hundreds or larger."

"You've been watching 'Police Story,'" Yoshiba said. "But you're right. I'll see if I can shake it loose for you."

"There's a feed bill," Heather explained.

"There's also three weeks' back rent at Billy's motel," Dave told her. "You didn't see anyone, hear anyone, after you shed Ace?"

She shook her head. "Was there someone?"

"There had to be someone, Heather," Billy said.

"There did not!" she snapped at him. "All there had to be was that boy Larry Johns. Yes—I saw *him.*" She shut her eyes a moment. "I'll never forget it."

"Are you absolutely sure Ace Kegan left the area?" Yoshiba tilted his head. "Up at the top of your driveway there are tire marks that indicate cars parked beside the road. He didn't drive up there and walk down the back way, here, so you wouldn't see him? He didn't get to your son before you did? You stopped to fix hot milk, remember?"

"Ace had shaken me. I'm aware I don't look as if anything could, but you've never had to deal with him when he's angry. I wanted to calm down before I confronted Rick."

"Should have had a drink," Billy Wendell grunted.

"So," Yoshiba began, "it's possible that Ace—"

"It is not!" she cried. "I heard the shot while I was climbing the stairs. Ace had driven off and Rick was dead when I got to the door of his room. I told you."

"You did," Dave said. "Was it true? Do you know why Lieutenant Yoshiba came with me this morning?"

"Because of you." The heavy old woman pulled herself into the saddle again. "Because you won't rest until you can involve me in my son's death. Or prove it was suicide. To save your company twenty-five thousand dollars. Which I'm sure it desperately needs."

"Wrong," Yoshiba said. "I'm here because you lied to me. Innocent people don't have to lie."

Billy Wendell snorted. "They do if they want to stay out of trouble."

Dave asked, "Why couldn't it have been suicide? He wasn't so humiliated when you burst in on him that he shot himself? It's been known to happen. Your kind of mother love can get to be too much to live up to."

Yoshiba jerked his head back, like a batter from a high inside fast ball. "What the hell does that mean?"

"It's abnormal psychology." Dave smiled thinly. "Not your field—remember?"

"It wasn't like that," Heather Wendell said stubbornly. "He was dead on the floor and Larry Johns was standing over him with the gun." She slapped the pinto's rump and it stepped out, startled, past the standing men. Billy Wendell nudged the sleek sides of the sorrel with the heels of cowboy boots that must also have belonged to his dead son. Nodding, the sorrel followed the paint.

"Not Ace Kegan?" Yoshiba asked.

Heather Wendell's back stiffened but she didn't answer. Above the clop of hoofs, she and her scarecrow ghost of a husband swayed on up the scabby drive, leather creaking. Yoshiba looked at Dave, shrugged, stepped off in their wake—not to follow them but to reach the car.

"Let's go find out," he said. "Who's the old joker?"

"Ex-husband," Dave said. "Father of the deceased."

"Back to cash in?" Yoshiba frowned. "Where was he?"

"Forget it," Dave said. "He was at a birthday party at a tavern in Torrance. For a long-lost small-time movie star named Lilian Drill."

"Who?" Yoshiba said.

"Sorry," Dave said. "Before your time."

Floor-to-ceiling curtains blinded the glass front of Ace Kegan's apartment. The deck was blanker than the beach. The sun had possession of both. But the sand had a few gulls and sandpipers. Yoshiba found a bell button in the redwood frame to the right of the glass sliding panels and pushed it. Nothing happened. He pushed it again. And a third time. Then there was sound from the apartment. Dave felt the deck shock faintly under him. The curtains jerked back. Kegan winced at them. His broken hands knotted the tie of a short gold velour robe. He clicked the lock on the aluminum doorframe and threw the panel aside.

"For Christ sake!" he said to Dave.

"Yes, early," Dave said, "right. This is Lieutenant Yoshiba of the Los Santos police."

Yoshiba looked at his watch. "It's after ten."

"I work till two," Ace Kegan said, "but if I didn't, I still wouldn't want to see you."

"We don't want to see you, either," Yoshiba said. "It's duty. You've heard of duty?"

Kegan said, "I told you to get him off my back." He glowered at Dave from under his lumpy brows. "Instead, you jump on too."

"And I'll tell you why," Yoshiba said. "You didn't tend bar at The Hang Ten Monday night. You sent your friend, there"—he nodded, Kegan turned, Bobby Reich dodged out of sight, Dave had an impression of blond nakedness and scared eyes—"to fill in for you."

Kegan's fists made clean, bumpy little clubs. He took a step. "Bobby!" he roared. A door slammed and no answer came. Kegan drew breath, turned back, working at a wry, broken-toothed smile. "All right. So Bobby filled in for me. It wasn't the first time."

"No, but it was the first time your partner got murdered," Yoshiba said. "And I doubt if you had dinner that often with his mother."

Kegan's mouth fell open a little.

"At the Hungarian place next to the theater where

she was supposed to be seeing a film in which they mistreated horses," Dave said.

Kegan gave a grim little laugh, pushed his hands into the pockets of the robe, turned away. "Okay. Come on in. I'll tell you all about it." He shouted, "Bobby, come and make coffee." He jerked his head at the long, shaggy white couch. "Move the books and sit down." He went into the kitchen and ran water. A kettle clattered onto a stove burner. He stood beside the bank of false flowers. "She was worried about Rick, afraid he was up to something."

"And she wasn't the only one," Dave said. "You told me he wasn't bright, that he didn't have any defenses, that he couldn't keep his mouth shut. Or words to that effect. Isn't that what you said?"

"You remember just fine," Kegan said.

"He'd talked to his mother about Larry Johns, hadn't he? After he'd first met the boy. That was why she was upset Monday. She'd recognized Johns's name when he gave it on the phone."

"She hoped he'd gone away," Kegan said. "Yeah, Rick met the kid in the bar—how long ago? Six weeks, couple months? Rick took him home. I wasn't supposed to know but Rick was clumsy. He sent the kid to wait for him up the beach at the all-night coffee stand and after we closed he picked him up in the VW. Just by watching him, I knew he was up to something. I followed him and I saw it happen. Next day, Rick was off his head, like the other times, with Monkey, with Savage. Couldn't talk about anything but Larry Johns. When the kid didn't come back, it died down. But Heather remembered."

"And so did you," Yoshiba said. "And we've got a witness that Johns gave his name when he called her to try to get hold of Wendell."

Kegan looked sourly at Dave. "All right, so he gave it. So I also knew there was going to be trouble. It doesn't change anything. We got together to talk it over, figure out a way to stop it."

"And you didn't waste any time," Yoshiba said.

"We decided to catch him *in flagrante delicto* and show him what a fool he was making of himself before it could go any farther."

"So you left the café without eating and each of you took your own car. Yours is a Fiat sports model, right? The new one parked in your space out back here?"

Kegan turned his head, wary, watching from the corners of his eyes. "Yeah. That's the one. I followed her. That was the first mistake. I could have been there ten minutes sooner. Then, when we did get there, she had to argue with me."

"Right. You had a fight at the foot of the stairs. She didn't trust you because you were too angry. She was afraid you'd hurt her son. She was also afraid of what you'd do to Johns. You made a lot of threats."

"He gets hysterical." Bobby Reich came out of the hall and went into the kitchen. He wore the white shorts.

"Oh, you're a real help," Kegan said.

"It's true." Bobby opened cupboards, rattled metal, crockery. "You know it's true. And why do you keep lying, Ace? They know all about it, you can tell."

"Deliver me from my friends!" Ace kicked a medicine ball. It rolled sluggishly a few inches on the thick white carpet. "Okay, I was boiling. And she got in my way. Christ, what football lost when Heather Wendell was born female! I couldn't get past her."

"She waited till you got back into your car," Yoshiba said, "and started the engine."

"But you didn't go home," Dave said. "You drove around back of the property, parked and—"

Kegan opened his mouth to protest.

"The tire marks are there," Yoshiba said. "Little Pirellis. Brand new."

"Mr. Moto lives." Kegan snorted disgust, wagged his head. "Yeah, little Pirellis. Okay, I parked and got out and went down the hill. Because I was damned if I thought she'd be enough. She might not even try. His sex life scared her. I was going to control my temper and it was going to work out like we planned. Only when I got down there I could see through the back windows. Rick was on the floor by the desk, Heather was holding a gun on the Johns kid and talking on the phone. Saying Rick was dead. There was no way I could help him. I'd only mess myself up. I got my ass out of there."

"Was the gun a surprise to you?" Yoshiba asked.

"I knew he had one. Heather made him get it. She had a fixation about hippies. They're thick up in that canyon and when the big dog died she wanted protection."

"Did you know where he kept it?" Yoshiba asked.

"Desk," Kegan said, "top drawer. He showed me."

"So it didn't shock you too much when you and Mrs. Wendell broke in on his lovemaking and he reached into the desk and came up with a gun. You were ready."

"He was dead on the floor when I got there," Kegan said. "Anyway, he'd never do that. Not to me."

"Never is a big word," Yoshiba said. "You rushed him to get the gun away from him and it went off, right?"

"Wrong," Kegan said. "I didn't even go inside."

"Does that road get a lot of use?" Dave asked. "That loop around in back of the Wendell place?"

"People go too far up the canyon—it's a way to get back out," Kegan said. "Kids used to park up there—to have sex. Heather used to go up with a big flashlight and try to run them off. But kids have changed. Lately they just laughed at her and went on fucking. So she phoned the police, let them handle it. I guess they did. She hasn't complained about it lately."

"Is that what you thought it was?" Dave wondered. "Necking kids? That car you found parked up there on Monday night?"

"I did?" Kegan turned, took coffee mugs from Billy, came at Yoshiba and Dave with them. He was frowning to himself. "Yeah. I did." He grimaced. "I didn't really notice. My mind was on Rick and Johns and Heather." He handed the mugs to the men on the couch. He looked at the sky-bright window wall. "But I don't think there was anyone in it. No.

157

Empty." He snapped his fingers. "Wait. They were down below the road. At least, he was." The boxer's broken face cracked a grin. "Yeah, I must have shook him. He ran like a rabbit. Back up to the road, right past me. Jesus!" Bobby came and handed him a steaming mug. He blew at it, chuckling. "What do you think? He left the girl there with her pants down under the trees in the dark?"

"What kind of car was it?" Yoshiba asked.

"Small." Kegan shrugged. "I don't know, didn't pay any attention. Besides, it was dark. I'd driven up with my lights off. So Heather wouldn't see."

"She heard a shot when she was climbing the stairs," Dave said. "You didn't hear it?"

"I might have," Kegan said. "It didn't register. Car isn't exactly quiet. I don't think so."

"Okay." Yoshiba set down his mug among the record albums and magazines on the table. He pushed his hard, square bulk up off the couch. "Thanks for the coffee." He began stepping over the body-building equipment, heading for the door. "I don't think you've got anything to worry about anymore. But keep yourself available. Don't take any sudden trips, okay?"

On the coast road, aiming back toward the Los Santos Civic Center, sun glinting off the curve of the windshield, Yoshiba said, "You didn't make it better, you made it worse."

"For Johns." Dave nodded glumly, slouched in the seat, staring without seeing at the flat blue surf. "Yes. I'm ahead of you."

"The kid is guilty as hell. And Larson's not going to have any trouble proving it. Not now."

"In his Little League cap?" Dave asked.

"He could wear a strait jacket," Yoshiba said, "and the jury would believe him. They'd have to. The kid laid down for Wendell for money. Then the money wasn't there. He attacked Wendell. Wendell tried to defend himself with the gun. It went off and Wendell was dead."

"That's not murder," Dave said.

"It's manslaughter," Yoshiba said, "and what you get for that is not a pat on the butt."

"I still don't believe it," Dave said.

"Fine," Yoshiba said, "but do me a favor, okay? Don't come to me with your doubts anymore. I'm busy, you know? Really busy."

13

Bulldozers chewed raw dirt flats out of brown-grass
summer hillsides where live oaks grew old and green.
The tire treads of graders, the cleats of rollers, stirred
yellow dust the wind took. Cement trucks climbed
dirt trails, tanks turning, turning, like pregnant iron
girls in sleep. Lower down the slope, racks of new
two-by-fours framed the shapes of houses to come.
Under a stand of tall and shaggy eucalypts, bench
saws whined and threw arcs of yellow sawdust into
the clean blue air. On plank rooftops, young men,
shirtless and sunburned, stapled down shingling
with guns that made quick, hard slapping sounds.
Hammers beat imperfect rhythms in the heat.

The silver Electra had brought Dave, air condi-
tioned, to the far and still nearly empty end of the
San Fernando Valley. He parked the car now next
to a long aluminum office trailer that waited this
side of the work area. A set of aluminum steps where
a lot of boot-scraping had taken place led to an
aluminum screen door. He stepped up, rapped the
doorframe, spoke to the darkness beyond the screen.
No one came. But he heard a scuff of shoes behind
him and turned. A bullish man walked toward him
in a scarred yellow hard hat.

"What can I do for you?"

"I'm looking for Elmo Sands." Dave stepped down and held out a card. "It's about Thomas Owens—the accident he had at his house on the beach at Los Santos."

The man's hands were busy managing blueprints the wind wanted to take away from him. He didn't reach for the card but he read it. It didn't appear to cheer him up. Still, he freed a hand to unlatch the screen door, nodded Dave inside and followed. He laid the blueprints on a long, crowded drafting table under fluorescent tubes in chain-hung flat white enamel reflectors. The blueprints began to curl up. The man stooped to an ice chest.

"I'm Sands. You want a beer?"

Dave didn't have a chance to answer. A cold, wet can was in his hand. The contractor hiked his barrel bulk onto a tin stool, thumbed the opener tab on his can and took a long pull at the beer.

"Ah, that's good. Really work up a thirst in this weather." He lifted off the hard hat and set it on the drawing table. Out of a damp mat of gray hair, sweat trickled down his leathery face. "Insurance, huh? Tom said he'd keep them off me. I told him it wouldn't work. I know insurance companies."

"They like to pay out money the way anyone else does," Dave said. "That was an expensive accident."

"Not my fault." Sands yanked a handkerchief from a hip pocket and mopped his face and neck. "That rail was bolted according to specifications. That's how I work—nothing gets overlooked. That's why

Tom Owens wants me. I've built every square foot he's designed since he went on his own. It's not that we're friends. He's got nothing but friends in this business."

"He said you don't make mistakes." Dave swallowed beer. "I'm willing to believe you both. But you personally can't set every bolt. You have people working for you." He nodded toward the sunny screen door, the sawing and hammering noises, the roar and complaint of machinery up the hills. "They can forget. Or just not give a damn. The facts say it happened. There were only loose nails stitching up that rail."

"Yup." Sands worked thirstily on his beer again. "I couldn't believe it and I went and looked."

"So it *was* your fault," Dave said.

"I thought so. And I fired the kid. I took him with me and showed him the nails and I fired him. He worshiped Tom. He couldn't face it that his carelessness had hurt the man. He got soaked through in the water around those rocks, trying to find those bolts."

"But he didn't come up with them," Dave said.

"He didn't come up with them." Sands took another quick pull at his beer, set the can down, began pawing among the papers and glints of blade and tooth on the drawing table. "He came up with this." He pulled out a thin, square, floppy magazine and held it toward Dave. It was the *Home* section of a Sunday Los Angeles *Times*. Even without his glasses, Dave recognized the color photo on the cover. It showed Tom Owens's dune house sharp-angled

162

against a sea sky streaked with sunset. "There's a two-page spread inside," Sands said.

Dave put on his glasses and turned pages. The stool gave a snap and creak of relief when Sands got off it to stand next to Dave, smelling of hops and Brut deodorant. Dave found the spread, text and five pictures, three of houses Owens had designed for film and television personalities, and two more of his own house. Sands's thick index finger tapped a small photo in the lower right corner. Tom Owens, gaunt, high-shouldered, and wearing a bright striped sarape and western hat, rested elbows on the deck rail above the tide rocks where he'd fallen and broken both legs. The caption read: *Nightly custom: architect Owens watches spectacular sunset from cantilevered outpost.*

Sands said, "Look at the date on that magazine."

The date was a week before the accident. Dave handed back the section, folded up his glasses, pushed them into a jacket pocket. "You've shown this to Tom?"

"Haven't found the time," Sands said. "But it wouldn't matter to him. He didn't blame me for what happened. You were the one I kept it for. I knew there'd be an insurance investigator around sooner or later."

"Actually," Dave said, "he'd be from another outfit—Sequoia. They're the ones sending him checks. I'll save you the bother, though. I'll be talking to them today. I'll tell them about the magazine."

"Another outfit!" Sands scowled. "Well, then, what the hell are you doing here?"

"A friend of Tom's has been accused of murder," Dave said. "Tom doesn't think he did it. The dead man was insured by my company. That's where I come in. But none of my leads has gone anywhere. I haven't helped Medallion. I'd begun to think I couldn't help Tom. Coming to you was a long shot."

"If it's for Tom," Sands said, "I want to help."

"I think you have." Dave tilted back his head to finish off the beer. By the door a small black-enamel barrel that had once held roofing tar now held trash. He dropped the can into it. "Thanks."

"It's something about the bolts," Sands said.

"About the bolts," Dave said, "and about an accident that wasn't an accident and a murder that I'm pretty damn sure was." He unlatched the screen, hinged the bright door outward, stepped down into hammer strokes of sun. He turned back. "I hope you rehired that workman."

"Hell, yes," Sands said.

A mile west of the Medallion tower on Wilshire, a low-slung building of narrow red brick whose flat roof was a rubble of white rock housed Sequoia Accident and Indemnity. A handsomely kept jungle of leather-leaved greenery grew against the walls. Inside, no one sat at the glossy reception room desk where a multibuttoned green telephone winked lights and softly buzzed. Dave went past into a square patio sheltered by a big rubber tree. Glass doors led off the patio into offices.

Dave found Johnny Delgado in a corner room where open-flap cardboard cartons on the floor suggested departure. The desk was strewn with folders. Delgado, a trim little man who was Sequoia's claims investigator, stood with his back to the door, a foot up on a brick indoor planter, elbow on knee, chin on hand, head bowed as if he were studying the lush greenery. Without turning, he said in a beaten voice:

"Don't say anything, Marie. Whatever you want, it's yours. I can't fight anymore. Certainly not face to face. Certainly not today. Just go away."

Dave said, "It's not Marie, Johnny."

Delgado lifted his head, straightened his back, put the foot down, turned. He didn't look trim anymore. Beard stubble darkened his hollow cheeks. His eyes looked burned out. His suit looked as if he'd slept in it, and nowhere clean. He twisted Dave a wry smile of apology but didn't step around the desk, didn't make an effort to shake hands. He just said, "Christ," to himself and dropped into the chair back of the desk and waved a hand at another chair. Dave took it and Delgado said:

"When you're a kid, you get the idea there's only one female of the species in the world. You can't wait to marry her. Then you think what she's giving you instead of just the sex anybody's entitled to is her life or something." He laughed without amusement. "Oh, there's giving going on, all right. Only you don't know it. You think you're collecting a home, some money, a future, a comfortable retirement. Then she springs it on you. You've been collecting, all right. But not for the both of you. For her, exclusively for her."

"It's California," Dave said.

Delgado grunted, bent to open a drawer, to bring out a bottle. Jack Daniel's. Built into the brick wall over his head were clock hands in black wood. They made the time only minutes past noon. But Delgado, with hands that shook, poured steeply from the bottle into clear plastic throwaway glasses, put the bottle out of sight again, pushed one of the glasses toward Dave, between the clutter of files. "And what's on *your* mind?" he asked. The tone was meant to be resentful but it was too tired.

"They're all after you, are they?" Dave asked.

Delgado drank. "There's a reason." His smile was wan. "I'm not doing any work." He shook his head like a man jarred. "I don't understand it, Dave. We were getting along fine. No change. Not in ten years. I still can't believe it." He shut his eyes and emptied the glass and shuddered. It was probably six straight ounces. "Never could have believed we'd split. And if I could have believed it, I sure as hell wasn't ready for what it's doing to me. I can't function." He pushed savagely at the files. "I can't even read these fucking things. You're just lucky I happened to be here today. I haven't been in this office three hours running, not in a month." He took out the bottle again. His bruised and sorrowing eyes flicked at Dave's glass but Dave hadn't touched it. Delgado refilled his own glass. "I should have knocked her up. That's what my old man says. Keep 'em pregnant and you'll keep 'em. In the old country a woman was fat and ugly after five years of marriage. Nobody else would

166

want her. That was how they did it." He drank again. "Repulsive, right?"

"Buried there"—Dave nodded at the files—"have you got reports on two accidents to a household on the beach in Los Santos? Owens? Ewing?"

Delgado squinted, pushed at his thick, expensively cut black hair, hunched forward, began shifting the folders around. He did it sweating, slow, as if they were too heavy for him. He pulled this batch out from under that batch, peered at labels, dropped the first bunch in another place, pulled a second batch. But he grew impatient after half a minute, slammed the last handful down. Papers slithered out of them and lisped to the thick carpet. "Christ, I don't know. When? What's it about?"

"Gail Ewing, the woman, owned a Vega that her daughter drove." He named the Sunday of the rock festival. "She ended up rolling down a hill into a tree in Topanga Canyon. The brakes had failed. Now . . . I've just come from the police garage. They said you hadn't been there. And I believe them. Because you're good at your job and even if you weren't, you couldn't have missed on this one. Johnny—there wasn't any brake fluid in the master cylinder."

"A leak?" Delgado frowned, rubbed his stubbly face.

"No leak," Dave said. "Somebody drained the fluid and didn't replace it."

"Car been in for repairs before that?"

Dave said, "Never. It was a new car and nothing had gone wrong with it to warrant a checkup."

Delgado groaned and finished off his drink.

"Why don't you stop that?" Dave asked. "Work will do the same thing. And you come out into daylight."

"Yeah, right." Delgado nodded. "Right, but too late. I'm out. I just got the word. Very kindly, very understandingly, but I'm fired. All I'm in here for is to get my personal stuff and get the hell out."

"One more thing and I'll leave you to it," Dave said. "This Ewing woman's brother, Thomas Owens, two days after the car accident, fell from a deck of his house that overhangs rocks in the surf and broke both his legs. The bolts that held the deck rail in place had been removed. I have proof."

Delgado for the first time looked out of his eyes, past the blur of pain. "I remember," he said. He glanced at the pile of folders. "They're not here. I signed them, Dave. I signed a lot of stuff. It was the second week. Everything had accumulated, like now. I just signed them all. I walked in here after receiving a very choice letter from my wife's attorney. And I was smashed and I sat down in this chair and I said, 'The hell with it,' and I took 'em all on. I didn't read 'em—I signed 'em, signed 'em all."

"That's costing Sequoia," Dave said. "Which doesn't much matter. What does matter is that somebody was trying to kill Thomas Owens. Both those times they missed. I think there was a third time. They missed Owens then too. But someone else got a bullet in the chest and died. It wouldn't have happened, Johnny—not if you'd looked at that car, looked at that deck rail."

Delgado was a bad color. "Get out of here," he said thickly. "Just get out, will you, please?"

The plank roadway that crossed the dunes to the stiff wooden sails of Tom Owens's house was too narrow for cars to pass on it. So when the Vega came out of the shadow of the port now, Dave braked the Electra and pushed the lever to Reverse. Then he saw Jomay's bright hair through the windshield and shifted to "N" instead and stepped out. Gail Ewing halted her car, tapped the horn, called sharply:

"We have a plane to catch!"

He walked to her. Larry Johns was in the cramped rear of the little car, where there was no room for his legs. He sat crossways on the fake leather seat, head pulled down to his shoulders to avoid the low ceiling.

"Where did you come from?" Dave asked.

"Tom got his lawyer on my case," Johns said. "Mr. Greenglass. It was only manslaughter if it was anything, he says, and that's not like murder, where they can hold you without bail."

"Legal technicalities had nothing to do with it," Gail Ewing snapped. "It was Tom's fifty thousand dollars. That was where the judge set bail—which shows you what he thinks of the case."

"It's not a case yet," Dave said. "And I'm not sure it's ever going to be."

"Doubt away," Gail Ewing said, "but right now I must ask you to move your car."

Dave looked across at Jomay. BB lay asleep in the girl's narrow lap, golden head between her little

169

breasts, rosebud mouth drooling on a fresh white blouse, probably one of Trudy's. Dave asked, "Back to Texas?"

Jomay nodded sulkily. "I give my statement about Huncie to that man in the baseball cap. They had it typed up. I signed it. They don't need for me to stay." She glanced bitterly at Gail. "I would have stayed. Tom—he says I'm more'n welcome."

"He gave you the fifteen hundred," Johns said. "That's what you come out here to get, isn't it?"

Jomay twitched her mouth, tossed her hair.

Dave asked Johns, "You're going to the airport to say goodbye? I thought you said goodbye in Austin fifteen months ago."

"I want to see that Delta jet take off," Johns said. "Watch it till it's out of sight."

Jomay turned sharply on the seat. "It was Mama drove you off," she yelled. "Wasn't that what you said? Makin' you clean up her beauty parlors and never payin' you? Now you talk like it was me you hate."

He sighed and said gently, "I don't hardly remember you, Jomay. Why don't *you* try that? Just forget me."

Jomay picked up the limp baby under its arms and shook it at him. "This here is yours!"

The baby began to cry and Johns turned his thin child face to look out the rear window.

"It's good flying weather," Dave told him. "The plane will get off all right. I'm sure Mrs. Ewing here will report back accurately. I need to talk to you. And Tom. There are some developments."

"For heaven sake!" Gail Ewing threw open the door, got out of the car, yanked the bucket seat forward against the steering wheel. "Get out if you're not going. We've got less than an hour now."

Johns half crawled, half fell out of the tight little car. Gail slid behind the wheel again, slammed the door, raced the engine. Dave returned to the Electra, backed it along the hollow-sounding planks to the wide place on the coast road shoulder where the drive began, swung it out of the way. The Vega shot past, Jomay's face flushed, BB still wailing. Her cries mingled with those of the gulls wheeling the emotionless blue sky above the dunes.

Dave rolled the heavy car to where Johns stood waiting, squinting up at the gulls, his hands in the hip pockets of the worn Levi's. They came into the house down stairs into the kitchen, where the dogs jumped and barked around Johns. He dropped his Levi's and the pumpkin-color dog snatched them and the others ran after him barking. Johns wasn't quite naked. He wore very small yellow swim trunks. He peeled off his T-shirt as he led the way along under the gallery to the room at the far house corner, where Tom Owens said from his hospital bed:

"Good—you didn't go."

He held out his arms to Johns, then saw Dave and dropped the arms and dropped his smile. It was the best smile Dave had seen in a long time and he hated to see it go.

"What is it?" Owens said. "Larry's free. Isn't that fine?" The boy perched on the bed edge. Owens stroked his shoulder. He cocked an eyebrow at Dave. "Aren't you pleased?"

"It's too early," Dave said. "I'll be pleased when they refund your bail money and he crosses home plate, but he hasn't crossed home plate—not yet. And that's only half of it. The other half is you."

"Me? I'm fine—now."

"You're a target," Dave said. "Someone tried to kill you. Not once but twice." He eyed the boy with the blond mustache. "And possibly three times." Owens tried to interrupt. Dave didn't let him. He told about the brake fluid, the deck bolts, about how Johnny Delgado had neglected his job, about how the kid who worked for Elmo Sands hadn't.

Owens was pale against his pillows. Reaching for cigarettes on the magazine- and book-strewn blankets, his hand shook. He fumbled the pack and dropped it. Larry Johns took it, lit two cigarettes from it, handed one to Owens. The architect looked bleakly at Dave. "That's right. The photographer posed me leaning on that rail. Backward and frontward. It was his idea."

"So the caption was fiction," Dave said. "You didn't go out there every night at martini time to watch the sunset."

"Sunsets," Owens said, "are usually in bad taste."

"But you fell off there," Dave said. "How?"

"Trudy and Mark were recording." Owens gave an ironic laugh. "I was minding their business."

"The night before," Dave asked, "you don't remember the dogs barking? Somebody was out there removing those bolts. It had to be under cover of darkness."

"We were catching a play at the Mark Taper—Larry and I. Gail?" He creased his forehead. "Where was she?"

"Free child-care centers for working mothers," Johns said. He squinted in the smoke from his cigarette, probing for and finding the brown pottery ashtray. "What would happen to Gail if she ever had to mind her own business for a week?"

Owens laughed without hope or humor. "The world would be up to its ears in stray infants and oil slicks." He frowned. "Mark and Trudy weren't home that night either. Where were they?"

"Poetry marathon," Larry Johns said. "At that far-out bookstore in Santa Monica. Ninety-nine poets, or something, reading steady for two days and two nights. The store wanted to get it in the *Guinness Book of World Records*. They used up about fifty tape cassettes and found out afterward the mike wasn't plugged in. Remember?"

This time Owens's laugh was real. "Yes—right."

Dave said, "So whether the dogs barked or not, there was no one home to hear them. How about when the brakes on your sister's car were tampered with?"

"That was no way to kill me," Owens said. "I never drive that car."

"That was on a weekend." Larry Johns tugged at the ragged ends of his blond mustache, frowning, thoughtful. "Maybe they weren't here. We left them for shots at the vet's one Saturday." He went to a file cabinet and brought Dave a slip of paper headed LOS SANTOS ANIMAL CLINIC. The scrawled date was right. Dave handed back the slip and the boy put it away again. Owens watched his thin nakedness. The yellow eyes smiled and looked hungry. Dave told Owens, "Madge Dunstan and Ray Lollard picture you as someone everybody likes. So does Elmo Sands. He says you have only friends."

"I'd have thought so," Owens said. "In that way, at least, I've always been lucky."

"Think. There's no one you've crossed?" Dave sat in one of the orange canvas director's chairs. "Suppose you hadn't come along—who would have built those expensive beach houses that made you famous?"

"Anyone and no one." Johns sat on the bed edge again and Owens stroked his back. "It really doesn't add up, Dave."

"Does Larry ever drive your sister's car?"

"No." Owens stopped his moving hand. "Gail and Trudy. Larry drives my car, the El Camino. What are you getting at?"

"You look alike—fair, slender, long hair, mustaches," Dave said. "And on the night Rick Wendell was killed, Larry wore your sarape and hat."

The two on the bed watched him, puzzled.

Dave told Johns, "Try to remember. We know now that Mark followed you that night. You evidently didn't notice him. Did you notice anybody else when you left the house and headed for the road where Wendell was waiting to pick you up?"

"No. But I went out the driveway. In my cowboy

boots. They made a lot of noise on the planks. If somebody went on the sand underneath I wouldn't have heard."

"And you didn't notice a car following you when you drove up into the canyon with Rick?"

"Tell you the truth"—Johns blushed scarlet, got off the bed, went to stand looking out the window— "Rick had kind of busy hands. Well, one hand, anyhow. A couple times I thought we'd go off the road."

"So you weren't watching the rear-view mirror. You didn't see the headlights of the El Camino that Mark was driving. You didn't see headlights from another car?"

"Sorry." Johns stepped to the bed to put ashes into the brown pottery tray. "What you think is the same one that tried to kill Tom by rigging those brakes and the deck rail came back and saw me leaving and mistook me for Tom and followed along to try to kill me?"

Owens, pale again, took the boy's hand, gripped it hard. He looked at Dave. "You think he went right into Wendell's place and that was what Larry heard and—"

"And that Wendell came out to investigate, found a stranger, snatched the gun from the desk, the stranger tried to get the gun away from him and it went off. Yes."

"Jesus," Johns whispered. "He saved my life."

"It was someone who didn't know me that well," Owens said with sudden conviction. "He tampered with the wrong automobile, then with that deck rail, where it was only by bad luck I happened to lean." He breathed in sharply. "He'd seen that magazine picture."

"And believed the caption," Dave said. "And you wore the sarape and hat. Also on television, right?"

"For color." Owens's smile was self-mocking.

"But you can't think of anyone who wants you dead." Dave got up grimly from the director's chair and went to the door with the high wall break above it. "Try, Tom. Give it hard thought. There's got to be someone. And if we don't find him, Larry isn't going to stay free."

Johns wasn't listening. Worried, he tugged at his mustache again. "Tom? They're running in a memorial to Rick at that Mr. Marvelous shuck tonight. I know Gail and the kids will be out. But I ought to go. I won't stay late. I mean—hell, he did save my life."

"A friend." Owens's voice was heavy with irony but his smile was kind. "Sure, go. I'll be all right."

"I couldn't go to the funeral," Johns explained.

"Don't sweat it," Owens said. "It's okay."

Watching them, the boy standing by the bed, the man in the bed holding his hand, smiling up at him, Dave had a sudden nightmare sense of déjà vu.

"Wear the sarape and hat," he said.

He left them staring blankly at each other.

14

Along a stretch of wide West Santa Monica Boulevard where the city criminal code didn't reach, signs, red, blue, yellow, flashed names at the rental cars of tourists that crawled past, bumper to bumper, while the Iowans inside, eyes circled by white from desert sunglasses, marveled. The signs read INSTITUTE OF ORAL SEX, DO IT MODELING STUDIO, PEEK IN ADULT BOOKS, PUSSYCAT THEATRE. In calligraphies of glass, GIRLS GIRLS GIRLS wrote itself on the wide black slate of the night sky—TOPLESS, BOTTOMLESS, GO-GO DANCERS, BOYS BOYS BOYS. TOTAL, the signs said, NUDITY. And there were neon drawings of gigantic naked hips and breasts and smiles.

Surprisingly, but only to those who didn't know Los Angeles, in the midst of all this loomed an old-time livery stable, newly painted red with white trim—THE BIG BARN. It was the largest L.A. gay bar, logical host to the Mr. Marvelous contest. Day-Glo banners fluttered on its country front. A swivel klieg light mounted on a noisy flatbed truck sent a blinding blue-white shaft into the high darkness. Barbra Streisand wailed from loudspeakers over an entryway lit by electrified ranch-house lanterns.

A strip of incongruous red carpet crossed the

sidewalk. At the curb, glossy rented limousines halted and discharged beautiful youths who looked nervous and a little too muscular for their hired tuxedos. The way traffic inched along gave Dave time to study them. He'd met the majority. But the clothes, the grooming, varnished them to sameness. And they hadn't glowed like this in their jeans and work shirts at the bars. Only Bobby Reich. Clothed or unclothed, Bobby dazzled. He stepped out now from Ace Kegan's shiny little Fiat.

A crowd five rows deep behind red silken ropes made a gantlet of the stretch from curb to door. They gasped and sighed. Camera bulbs flashed. Microphones glittered toward smiling mouths like drunken missiles toward the moon. A bored-looking man with a motion picture camera saddling a shoulder pushed onlookers. Dave reached a corner and idled up a side street where the dense leafage of old acacias dimmed the street lamps. He was three blocks off before he found a parking space that would take the Electra.

When he got back to The Big Barn, the crowd was funneling inside. Ahead of him, he glimpsed the cheap red windbreaker and childlike brown hair of Vern Taylor. When he himself got inside and handed money to a rosy-cheeked boy-man in the oiled and hand-rubbed horse stall that was making shift as a box office, Dave turned to search the press of men and boys behind him. In the doorway stood Kovaks and Ray Lollard—Lollard beaming with pride and joy, Kovaks unshaven, in clay-stained bib overalls. Dave chuckled. It was to Lollard he had mailed Kovaks's gift pot. Tonight at dinner with Madge, Doug had told him that Kovaks was moving his workshop into the carriage house back of Lollard's old mansion.

The main room of The Big Barn was enormous, propped by splintery posts and overhung by haymows. The wired barnyard lanterns glowed everywhere, amber mostly but sometimes red and green, now and then even white. Sawdust was thick underfoot. Sets of spurs, cracked oxen yokes, lariats coiled and lacquered into uselessness, hung against the walls. Dave's foot kicked a brass spittoon. Strictly ornamental—it sprouted plastic flowers. This was the West—but only West L.A.

On the room's far side, long mirrors in old mahogany frames, probably bought on the back lot of some defunct film studio, reflected glittering bottles. Maybe he could get a drink. He began muttering excuses and using a shoulder and an elbow. In five minutes he had reached the long bar that matched the mirrors. Brunswick would probably have been the manufacturer's name but too many elegantly clad pelvises were in the way—he couldn't look for the label.

He had to wait awhile but a double Scotch came to him at last. It tasted like a prescription by a dropout pharmacist. But the commingled smells of strong colognes around him overpowered the taste and he drank it. He felt himself grin at the painting above the bar. No buxom Gay Nineties lady on a tufted red velvet sofa but cowboys taking each other's Levi's off in a moonlit bunkhouse—cowboys pretty as girls and hung like stallions. A voice at his ear said:

"I haven't seen you in here before."

Dave didn't look around. "Just passing through," he said. "As quickly as possible."

The owner of the voice turned away. "You're right—she's vice."

"Vice?" someone else said. "Impossible. She's wearing matching shoes."

A change came in the dense warp and weft of talk that stretched across the huge room. He glanced at his watch, then looked toward the end of the place where spotlights fingered down. There on a makeshift stage under the planking of a loft, a slim man in a white tuxedo, shirt ruffles, a silver wig sprinkled with mica, clutched a chrome microphone stand. A sunburst of colored foil backgrounded him. On a table beside him three brass trophy cups gleamed above watches and cuff links in jewelers' boxes and a display by an expert window dresser of shirts, sweaters, pants, jackets.

The man on the stage moved his mouth but no sound reached across the wide blue lake of tobacco smoke. Laughter and shouts pelted him. *We can't hear you, Vic, darling!* He visored his eyes with a hand on which rings sparkled. He peered toward the darkness beyond the end of the stage. Suddenly, electronic feedback howled through the room. There were shrieks. Then, "Welcome!" came from the man in white. It came too loud and folded back on itself in a ringing echo. He stepped away from the mike, laughing, put a hand on his hip and squinted into the darkness again. He tried again. And this time all was well—or as well as could be expected.

"Welcome to the Third Annual Mr. Marvelous Awards! I'm your host, Vic Waverly. These have always been superb evenings. This one will top them all, I promise you, my dears. From the point of view of entertainment, from the stunning quality of the men—and I lay stress on that word, oh, do I lay stress on that word, darlings!—who have become finalists in the competition. You'll meet them in a minute. But first, I want to ask the judges to stand up so you can meet them. They're distinguished members of the Southern California Gay Community. Taking them in alphabetical order—"

First was a minister, complete with dog collar, though he'd got his training in backwoods Baptist seminaries in the deep South. Next was a moon-faced man with a belly who had begun as a gay activist at fifty after a lifetime of bailing out likely youths from jail, and now spent his nights on television talk shows explaining the gay mystique, whatever that was. Last was an acne-scarred publisher who served the homosexuals of fifty states with a sleek magazine that glamorized sadism and Texas mass murderers. There wasn't much applause but Dave knew better than to be gratified—the reason was, everyone held drinks and glossy program books.

Music came through loudspeakers. Hawaiian, of all things. Dave flinched, tilted up his glass, found only ice and asked for another drink. While he waited he ran a troubled look over the room again. And smiled grim satisfaction to himself. There was the white Stetson, the gaudy sarape. He dropped bills on the counter, picked up his glass. The time had come to move. If there was going to be action, he didn't want anyone hurt. Or dead. He began shouldering his way with apologies through the crowd.

But when he reached the spot by a post with fake cattle brands burned into it where he'd seen Larry Johns, the boy wasn't there. Dave pushed on, craning to get another glimpse of the hat through the acres of fashionable haircuts, edging and jostling first to one side of the room, then the other. He ended up in an open area in front of the stage. It surprised him. There were even empty chairs, two rows of the folding kind, gray metal tubing, white padded plastic seats. They faced the backs of the judges, huddled over charts and photographs.

A fat little black-bearded man hung with straps and leather cases crouched, flashing camera bulbs at them. Behind the stage more bulbs flared. This space, these chairs, were for the press, of course, when they finished with the shiny-headed contestants back there and the gray-headed managers. Dave glimpsed Ace Kegan's knotty hands fidgeting with Bobby's tie. Dave dropped onto a chair and lit a cigarette. Maybe Larry Johns would find him. But it wasn't Larry Johns who touched his shoulder. He turned and looked up into the silver-marred smile of Vern Taylor. Taylor said:

"I saw you come in and I was pretty surprised. I mean, I knew you were gay—I can always tell. But I didn't think you'd come for this. I thought your life style would be different. You'd have a lover, somebody permanent. And you'd go places like ballets and operas and plays and art galleries. Together. You wouldn't cruise bars like this, and baths, and all that."

"I'm working," Dave said. "Still trying to find out about Tom Owens's accident."

Taylor didn't answer. He eyed Dave for a moment, then looked at the stage. So did Dave. A trio of slim little Polynesian youths, brown, sleek, smiling, had come out of the dark. They were wrapped to the waist in bright missionary cotton. Their small hands did graceful flower-in-the-wind turns, their narrow hips twisted dreamily. Taylor made a sound. Dave looked at him. His eyes were bright. He licked his lips.

The tempo of the tune quickened. As one, the boys gave slow winks. Slowly, not missing a beat or a gesture, they turned their backs. Slowly their hands found the cloth knots at their sides, twitched them, and the bright print wraparounds dropped. They were naked. Whoops. Whistles. They waggled little brown butts and, still keeping time with the music, slowly turned to face the crowd. Cheers. Jeers. Someone shouted, "My God, it's an invasion of field mice!" The boys joined in the laughter.

Dave turned to check Taylor's reaction but Taylor had moved off. The red jacket showed among a knot of people that had formed where steps came off the side of the stage. But Taylor wasn't watching the dancers. He was watching Dave. From here he looked about sixteen. Except for his expression.

Dave didn't know what it meant. Startlement but something else too—something ugly. And the look wasn't at him. It was at something past him. He turned. Larry Johns stood there, not sure how much to smile, fingers nervous at his ragged young mustache. He plucked at the bright sarape.

"I did like you asked," he said. "I don't know why."

Dave stood. Maybe simply to shield the boy from that basilisk stare of Taylor's. He said, "Your photo was in the *Times*. Evidently before Yoshiba got you away from there, reporters came. You were on those long cement stairs down from the Wendell place. Wearing that outfit."

"Yeah." Johns's clear brow wrinkled. "So?"

"Have you thought," Dave asked, "why someone tried three times to kill Tom—then didn't try anymore?"

"Oh, wow." Johns sat down as if maybe his legs were unsteady. He watched the bare brown boys a moment without really seeing them. He blinked at Dave. "No, not really. It's kind of funny, though, isn't it?"

"I hope it stays funny," Dave said. "But I'm betting it won't. Keep close to me—right?"

"What's wrong?" Johns looked around, alarmed.

"Take it easy," Dave said. "I'm working on a hunch. They're not always reliable."

The music reached a final whining upslide of guitars, the brown boys snatched up their fallen sarongs and fled the stage, giggling like the three little maids from school. Applause clattered off the wooden walls. For this, people had abandoned their drinks. Confetti showered from the lofts. A few colored balloons wagged toward the high, shadowy rafters. Someone on a loft reached out and punctured one. It popped like a shot.

The man in the white tuxedo returned, applauding, to the microphone. "Our thanks," he said, "to the management of The Flower Lei for sending us Mei Mei, Tei Tei and Laverne." Laughter. "Seriously, if that didn't get you in the mood, lie down, dears—you're dead. All right. So much for foreplay." Laughter, his own with the crowd's. "Now, I know you're all dying for a look at the stars of the evening—those handsome and talented and sexy finalists for the title 'Mr. Marvelous.' What?" He turned from the mike, stepped toward the back of the stage. "Yes, right." He faced the crowd again. "They're ready—isn't that nice? They've only had four months. Anyway—take a good look at them with their clothes on. It will be your last chance tonight." Cocked eyebrow, open hand on breast. "Did I say that? All right—here we go. First, from The Barracks, contestant number one, Skeets McIntyre—five eleven, one sixty, actor, bronco buster, Texan from top to toe. Let's hear it for Skeets McIntyre!" He backed from the microphone, applauding. McIntyre appeared in the spotlights. His eyes were too close together.

The parade ran on while the smoke thickened and the comments of the M.C. thinned and the judges squinted upward appraisingly and made notes with chewed pencils. The biggest applause came for

Bobby Reich. But as Dave understood it, appearance was only a step. Somehow or other, as the evening wore on, talent and intelligence were supposed to be displayed. He set his drink between his feet on the sawdust and applauded Bobby. It might be his only honest opportunity. More balloons were loosed. Two of them banged this time. He wished that would stop. Here was a hairy lad in skin-tight wet-look black plastic from The Rawhide. And last, a lissome prince—princess?—from The Queen and Court.

He reached down for his glass and nearly bumped heads with Ace Kegan, who was crouching in front of him, trying to make himself heard over the din of clapping, cheering, stamping, music, the clatter of empty beer cans underfoot. At the same moment, Dave noticed Vern Taylor trying to come back, working his way past the knees and floor-tangled camera cases of the news people who now filled the chairs. Except that no one filled the chair next to Dave. Where the hell was Larry Johns? Dave bent toward the broken face of the little ex-boxer. If this was bad news about Bobby Reich, then his worries about this evening were off target. He cupped a hand to his ear. But what Kegan said was:

"You're wanted on the phone. By luck I was there when the call came. They won't page anybody—not with a crowd like this. Too many people afraid the boss might learn where they were. But I heard the dude who took the call speak your name. It's some kind of emergency. Somebody's mother. Otherwise I wouldn't have bothered. You don't exactly top my list of people I want to do favors for." He got to his feet, jerked his chin. "Phone's back of the bar."

"Thanks." Dave stood, pushed his chair aside, headed for the mirrors. While he fought his way, he squinted around him, trying to locate Larry Johns. Nowhere. He swore to himself. The phone receiver lay like a stunned thing by a silver-painted wrought-iron cash register halfway along the back bar. Dave worked the trick latch of the gate at the bar's end. A hefty youth in a leather vest and waxed mustaches blocked his way. He gave his name. The youth went back to the tall, spooled spigot handles and the foaming steins he was supposed to be minding. Dave picked up the phone.

"Get to the pet store, will you?" It was Doug. "On the double, please. Dave, she's really done it this time. She's liberated everything. The God damn sky is alive with parakeets and cockateels. Rabbits, guinea pigs, hamsters, white rats down every storm drain, cats and monkeys up every tree. They were political prisoners. She's Secretary General of the U.N. or something. Declared a worldwide general amnesty. I got the turtles back and a couple of toads. I'm quicker than they are. And, thank God, she didn't think of the fish. Yes, the fire department's coming. And the S.P.C.A. They say. But I need *you*."

While he listened, Dave watched the stage. The pastor of gay sheep came to the microphone. His sweet, swamp-water tones met a hush of beery reverence. Head thrown back, eyes closed, hands folded demurely at his crotch, he told God what had happened to big, gentle, lovable Rick Wendell. As if God let cases stack up on his desk like Johnny Delgado. The prayer ended. An electronic organ with bronchial problems and a subnormal pulse began "The Lord's Prayer." A plump, balding young man stepped up to sing the words.

And a gun went off. Not that near, but near. The sound was nothing like the bursting of balloons. Bad nerves had tricked his memory. The crowd didn't know the difference. The organ and the off-key baritone wobbled on and they listened. But Dave knew the difference and felt very sick. Larry Johns. Why had he wandered off when Dave had warned him? Where was Vern Taylor? Why had Doug's disaster had to happen now? He told the phone, "Doug, I can't. Not now. I'm sorry." He blundered the receiver into place and ran.

He didn't bother with apologies now, plowing his way backstage. He ended bruised and with a torn jacket pocket by the time he got there. In dim amber light, the contestants were stripping down to swim trunks. Silent. Out of respect for dead Rick Wendell and their own stage fright. The Big Barn's owner, bony, bucktoothed, sixty, in a silver-braided baby-blue satin cowboy outfit, was running an electric shaver over the bulging chest of his champion. Tenderly. Dave took it away from him, thumbed the switch to stop the waspish little motor, pushed the shaver into the boy's hand, took the man's stringy arm, led him away.

"There's been a shooting," Dave said quietly. "Out in back, I think. How do we get there?"

The man blinked, went pale, swallowed hard. But he moved. He led the way around a plank-and-stud partition that made a kind of hallway. To one side, doors were labeled US and THEM. There was a zinc-covered kitchen door with no light, no activity behind it. At the end of the hallway, a red EXIT sign was dim over a door with many bolts and chains. They weren't fastened. The bucktoothed man pulled the door open. The bulb outside was even dimmer, forty watts in a cage. It threw more shadow than light. There were big, scarred trash modules, stinking galvanized-iron garbage barrels, crates filled with smashed bottles. And in a chain-link fence corner clotted with soggy wastepaper—a man. He lay face down in a puddle that showed rainbows of oil. And something darker. Blood.

"My God!" The bucktoothed man put out a hand.

Dave knelt by Ace Kegan, laid fingers against the big vein in his neck. Life still beat there. But no thanks to Dave. Anger churned in him, disgust. Granted there'd been a lot of ways to be wrong in this case—did he have to try them all? And always too late? He got to his feet. "He's not dead," he told the bucktoothed man. "Phone the police. They'll bring an ambulance."

"What are you going to do?"

"I'm going to the beach." Dave headed for the glare of neons at the end of the alley. "As fast as I can get there. I hope to God it's fast enough."

15

But Hollywood traffic on a summer weekend night was geared down. There was no way to get through it fast. In a three-block-long jam-up that had lasted through ten minutes of signal changes, he got disgusted. He left the car idling in the middle lane near La Cienega and Santa Monica and closed himself in a telephone booth. It stood against the curved stucco wall of a topless dance place. It smelled of marijuana smoke. He dug in his pocket. And the coins were wrong. Many yards off on an opposite corner, a Rexall drugstore promised change. There wasn't time. The signal went green. Horns began to blare behind the abandoned Electra. He dodged back to it. It was his turn at last and he made it across Santa Monica, but the achievement meant nothing. Down the long slope of restaurant row, the traffic clogged forever. When after another five minutes he reached a side street, he swung west toward Robertson. He'd phone from the apartment.

He sat on the bed, sweating, working his way out of his jacket, tugging down the knot of his tie, and listening to the phone buzz busy at Tom Owens's end. He tried twice more. Hopeless. He lit a cigarette and dialed Operator. His shirt was soaked. The night breeze through the big empty rooms made him shiver. "Look, I'm trying to reach this number." He gave it. "And it's busy. Can you break in on the line? It's urgent."

"One moment—I'll give you the supervisor."

The supervisor took more than a moment. And when she did get around to him, it didn't help. "I'm sorry. That number is out of order. I'll report it."

"Oh, no!" Dave said. "Look, the party's an invalid. Maybe he knocked the phone off the hook."

"I wouldn't be able to give you that information," she said. "You'd have to call Repair Service. They can check it for you. Dial 611."

He dialed it and it rang a long, long time, but they checked the phone. "It is off the hook, sir. If this is an emergency, we can use a howler on it."

"Great," Dave said. "Make it a loud howler."

"They're not very loud," the girl said. Whether it was or not, Tom Owens didn't seem to hear it. "No one answers," the girl said.

"Right, thanks." Dave hung up and bent to twist out his cigarette in the ashtray on the floor. Hell, he'd only wasted time. What good would it do to warn Tom Owens someone was coming to kill him? He couldn't move from that bed. Dave dialed another number.

"Los Santos police. Officer Zara speaking."

Officer Zara didn't sound more than sixteen.

"Lieutenant Yoshiba, please. Dave Brandstetter calling. It's an emergency."

"I'm sorry, sir. He's not here. Matter of fact, I'm

the only one that is here. If you're calling about the trouble in Paradiso—"

"I wasn't. What's the matter?"

"It's the college kids again. They're trashing the mall again. They've occupied a bank. They're burning it. And somebody's sniping at the police. Everybody's there." He sounded wistful, left out.

"Well, look, Officer Zara," Dave said. "I have reason to believe there may be an attempt at homicide. The Thomas Owens house." He gave the R.F.D. address on the coast road. "Can you send somebody? The man's alone there, laid up in bed, legs in casts."

"He hasn't called us," the boy said.

"He doesn't know the danger he's in," Dave said. "And while we're talking—"

"Okay, sir. I understand. I've written down the address. I'll try to radio a car, send them out there. He's alone like that? No nurse?"

"No nurse. The whole family's away tonight."

"What about dogs? Those people out on the dunes, they usually have a dog."

"Right," Dave said. "They've got dogs."

The big dog lay just inside the open front door. It lay on the polished floorboards among splinters of glass. A panel had been smashed out of the door. Dave crouched by the dog. The light was poor. It came a long way—from the hanging wicker lamp above the wicker furniture at the room's far end. But it was enough to show him a puddle of drying blood under the dog's head. He touched the motionless body. It had begun to lose heat in the cool beach night, begun to stiffen. The fur had lost its sheen and felt coarse. There was no sign of the other dogs.

A breeze sighed across the sand outside. There was the splash and sibilance of surf. Somewhere in the house, as in a ship, a beam creaked. He stood. And then he heard it, the sound of a voice. It came from beyond that far bulkhead, insistent, on a single pitch, no shift in tempo. It sounded not quite sane. But he knew the voice.

If he'd had any doubt about whom he was chasing out those red-taillight-streaked miles of freeway and coast road after escaping the tangle of city traffic, the doubt had been wiped out by what he'd found, a minute ago, leaking oil on the clean planks of Tom Owens's otherwise empty carport. It was a battered ten-year-old European mini. The slatted engine cover at the back was still hot.

Now he pried off his shoes and went quietly along beside the great painting under the gallery. Toward that edgy voice. The boxy hall the other side of the bulkhead was dark below but light came out through the tall opening above Tom Owens's closed door. It went high into a roof peak windowed by dark triangles of glass. The voice went up there too. And banged back down to Dave in the dark.

". . . Makes you want to vomit, doesn't it? Just hearing about it. Well, I lived it—two years of it, five months, eleven days. And you know why? Because once you get busted, they never leave you alone. They watch you all the time and they grab you.

Make a mistake nobody else would notice and they grab you. Also, you have a record. You can't get a job."

"Vern," Tom Owens said patiently, "I'm sorry. Why didn't you tell me all this the other day? Hand me the phone. I'll get you a job right now."

"It's too late. Anyway, that's not what I wanted from you. I asked you for all I ever wanted from you that summer when we were seventeen. You remember. At the Cahuenga Park pool. To go on the way we had been, Tommy, the way you started us. Don't forget, it was your idea. You were the oldest."

"Vern, it was a long time ago. Forget it. All right, yes. What I did to you was heartless and I'm sorry. But, Vern, I was only a kid."

"Sure, you're sorry," Taylor sneered, "with my gun at your head. Anyway, do you think 'sorry' can wipe out seventeen rotten years? Hell, I didn't care if you took up with Nofziger and those guys with cars and rich parents. Even when they called me fag. Even when you did. All I asked was for you to save a little time for me."

Owens interrupted. For a minute they both talked at once and the echo off the high boards of the hall broke the words and Dave couldn't understand them. Then Taylor was saying:

"I smell like flophouses, cheap bars, public toilets. I can't get clean. And you—you came out all shining. Let me tell you about this gun. I bought it on Main Street in L.A. From a black guy who hustles TV's— not machines, hustlers that dress like women. He sold it to me for five dollars. I walked out of the Ricketts Hotel after I saw you on the lobby television. I bought a gun to kill you with, Tommy."

Dave put his hand on the doorknob.

Owens said, "But you didn't use it. Instead you drained brake fluid out of the car, hoping I'd crash. Then you took the bolts out of the deck rail, wanting me to fall."

"I remembered bullets can be traced," Taylor said. "But you didn't die. It would have been on the news. It wasn't. So I came back. With the gun. At night. I waited out on the dunes because the lights were on. And then I saw you leaving. Only it wasn't you, just that boy in your clothes, only I didn't know that, it was too dark out there. He got in a car on the road and that big man kissed him and I thought, *I'll kill them in bed together.* Can you understand that, Tommy?"

"He was killed with his own gun," Owens said.

"I dropped mine," Taylor said. "He heard it. That was why he came out. And I ran at him and—"

"So you haven't used your gun," Owens said. "You can't be traced. Why don't you just—"

"Not shoot you?" Taylor jeered. "Sorry, but I have used it. Tonight. There were a lot of people around that old house. A kid outside the windows with a tape recorder. A big man in a cowboy hat. When he came, the kid ran up in the trees where I was. So close I could smell him sweating. He went after the big man went but there was someone else. A little man with a broken nose. When I ran back up to my car, I almost bumped into him. And he

was at that Mr. Marvelous contest tonight. He saw
me and he went straight to tell that insurance man,
Brandstetter. I had to kill that little man, Tommy."

"But now Brandstetter knows," Owens said.
"Vern, it's time you gave up. It's all going wrong."

"It always did," Taylor said. "For me. Everything
always went wrong. It didn't seem so bad when I
saw in the paper how they were holding that boy
for murder. I knew what he must be to you. That's
why I came to see you that day, Tommy. To watch
you crying for him the way I used to cry for you.
But he's out. I saw him tonight. I ought to have
known he wouldn't stay locked up. You had money
to get him out. Money can buy anything. There was
only one way somebody like me could hurt somebody like you. Kill you and—"

Tires rumbled heavily on the driveway planks.

"What's that?" Taylor asked.

"My family's come home," Owens said. "You can
still get away, Vern. Go out by the stairs just around
the corner. Out there in the hall."

"No!" Taylor said. "I'll kill them all. They mean
something to you. I never could, but they do. Maybe
I won't even kill you, Tommy. I'll kill them instead,
and you can live the rest of your life knowing you
caused it."

Rubber-shod footsteps made the floor shake.
Dave let the doorknob go, flattened himself against
the dark wall. The door opened. Taylor moved
toward the livingroom. Dave moved after him, silent,
swift.

Far off, at the foot of the stairs that spiraled

wooden down from the gallery, a door opened, brightness streamed out, then the long shadow of Larry Johns in the sarape and hat. "Tom?" he called. "Whose car is that up there? What's the matter with Hans and Fritz? They're out on the dunes and they won't come. They—" He broke off, ran to the dog, knelt. "Barney! Barney?" He touched the dead body, drew his hand back. "Aw, no, no!" He looked up.

And Taylor lifted a little nickel-plated revolver. Light slipped orange along its barrel. Dave struck Taylor's arm down. The gun spat fire and a bullet drew a groove in a polished floor plank. Taylor half turned. Dave chopped him across the windpipe with the edge of a hand. The gun clattered away. Taylor dropped, making a hoarse, rasping sound, clutching his throat, trying to take bites of air.

Larry Johns stood by the dead dog, staring, while Owens called from the next room, "Larry, are you all right? For Christ sake, Vern, what have you—?"

"It's all right!" Larry shouted. He came running down the room to Dave, careful to side-step the gun. He eyed the gun as if it were a snake. He looked uncertainly at Dave. "Isn't it all right?"

"As it's ever likely to be," Dave said. "Where did you disappear to at The Big Barn?"

"The men's room," Johns said. "Sorry."

Dave grunted. He touched the twisting, gasping Taylor with a foot. "Find something to tie him up with. He may be on our hands for a while. The police are busy tonight." He retrieved the gun, dropped it into a pocket. "I'll phone them again."

"Brandstetter?" Owens called.

Dave walked into the shiny plank room, picked up the phone from where it had spilled on the floor. "How did this happen?" he asked, and began to dial.

"I must have knocked it off in my sleep. It woke me, making a squawking sound. I couldn't reach it."

"Sorry about that." While at the other end of the line the phone rang and rang, Dave looked at the strung-up casts on Owens's legs. They were painted with flowers, bright primary colors, kindergarten draftsmanship. LOVE, in happy, drunken letters. "Was that how you spent the afternoon," he asked, "when you were supposed to be remembering someone you crossed once, someone with a grudge against you?"

The taut skin of Owens's high cheekbones reddened. He gave a sheepish nod. "Larry did it. We were celebrating his being back." He shook his head. "Seriously—I couldn't think of anyone."

"There's always someone," Dave said.

And officer Zara answered the phone.

If you enjoyed this novel, we think you'll like the other books in the Dave Brandstetter series:

Fadeout
Death Claims
The Man Everybody Was Afraid Of
Skinflick
Gravedigger
Nightwork
The Little Dog Laughed
Early Graves
Obedience
The Boy Who Was Buried This Morning
A Country of Old Men